John Hill

Wild Rose

Vol. I

John Hill

Wild Rose
Vol. I

ISBN/EAN: 9783337053383

Printed in Europe, USA, Canada, Australia, Japan

Cover: Foto ©Andreas Hilbeck / pixelio.de

More available books at **www.hansebooks.com**

A Romance.

BY

JOHN HILL.

'Sah ein Knab' ein Röslein stehn,
Röslein auf der Heiden,
War so jung und morgenschön,
Lief er schnell es nahzusehen,
Sah's mit vielen Freuden
Röslein, Röslein, Röslein roth
Röslein auf der Heiden.'

J. W. v. GOETHE.

IN THREE VOLUMES.

VOL. I.

LONDON:

TINSLEY BROTHERS, 8, CATHERINE STREET,
STRAND.

1882.

Dedicated

TO MY FRIEND,

E. S. C.,

WHO APPRECIATES

WILD ROSES.

CONTENTS OF VOL. I.

WILD ROSE.

CHAPTER I.

PRELIMINARY.

IT was early in the morning one September some years ago, during the first decade of the Second Empire, in the Boulevard St. Michel, in Paris; early enough for industrial and professional Paris only to be awake or astir. Workmen, robust, rubicund and sun-tanned, in blouses, were going in that leisurely conversational style peculiar to workmen when going toward their task—to build, to found and to destroy in the world of stone and

cement, minute particles of the latter rest-
ing on the black bristles of their unshaven
cheeks, serving as an unmistakable trade-
mark.   Cabmen and carters were standing
in the doorways or leaning on the zinc-
covered counters of Commerces des Vins,
talking and pondering, in all probability, on
the inadvisability of ever doing work, and
critically watching the laden tramcars that
jingled ponderously past them, bearing
other workmen, clerks and the like, whose
work was on one side of the Seine, and
their abode on the other.   Neatly dressed
girls, inheritors of the position of the now
extinct grisettes, were walking toward their
sewing-rooms, cigar counters, or other and
manifold scenes of labour, carefully avoid-
ing the puddles of the night's production,
which the sun, shining through a washed
blue sky, with white clouds storm-torn
like combed-out wool, had as yet not the
strength to efface.   It could display stains,

discolorations, and defilements, but, like
many a reformer, stopped at that, not
having the power or energy to remove
them. The Seine itself was a misty
mirror, fading into aërial perspective, with
each further bridge and tall pile of old city
buildings looking more hazily mysterious
than the nearer. The mist was over the
surface of the water everywhere, and
seemed like the breath of sleeping Paris.

Pleasure-seeking Paris was asleep—industrious, discontented, revolution-making
Paris was, as usual, wide awake; but the
time had not arrived for the latter to
strangle the former as it slept, and pay off
old debts so.

The Boulevard St. Michel is, as the
reader to whom Paris is familiar well
knows, one of those large, new and rigid
roads of the south side of the river, diverting and collecting the dark and crowded
streams of people from the dark and crowded

main arteries of the Quartier Latin, such
as the Rue, St. Jaques, or the Rue de la
Harpe. The Boulevard St. Germain is
just such another, nearly at right angles to
it. These two are the forerunners of the
great work of destruction so ably begun
under Napoleon III., and other rulers and
their talented advisers, destined ultimately
to eliminate antiquity and picturesqueness
from the Latin Quarter (which they now,
with their mathematical and statistical
precision choose to split into the Arron-
dissements du Panthéon and du Luxembourg), and with them the oldest historical
streets, and the shades of the great departed—Musset, Mürger, Mimi Pinson,
et hoc genus omne—and all the literary
and romantic halo which the mighty
and the darling dead have left behind
them. They are gone. Their memory
clings to the dear, dirty, tall old streets.
Why not leave them for one generation

more at least, till we have all been turned, by compulsory education and modern utilitarianism, into mathematicians, moralists, and meddlesome monomaniacs of sanitary reform, ready to sacrifice all beauty and poetry to remodelled drainage, and all artistic irregularity and Gothic quaintness to canons of art, in which every element of art except rigid perspective is omitted?

It is possible that the engineers or architects of the old streets drew the designs when their hands were in a state of bibulous tremor, and that the workmen faithfully copied the pattern (both of architecture and conduct therewith). It is possible that they showered down chimneys out of a supernatural and Brobdignagian pepper-castor, letting them stick where they would on the roofs, totally irrespective of the needs of the coal-consuming population below them, thus obliging these last to bore holes in the walls, and stick

black tubes through to let the smoke out,
and thus giving extra opportunites for
sentimental sufferers to suicidally suffocate
themselves. It is possible that drains were
as the mystery of iniquity and the abomi-
nation of desolation to these mediæval
constructors. Still, face to face with these
mighty and manifold faults, which a
carping criticism could carry further, and
indefinitely multiply, an irresistible, un-
reasonable and unreasoning affection, like
that of man for woman, unites those who
know the quarter, or what remains of it
through its poetic past, to that region of
learning and love, gaiety and despair,
fame and destitution, poetry and painting,
folly and vice, kindness and brotherly
affection, and eternal romance, on the south
side of the Seine.

In the Boulevard St. Michel, in the
midst of the said region, are many cafés
and brasseries, patronised mainly by the

students of the University, and the miscellaneous literary and artistic population of the neighbourhood. These are different from the cafés to which you, wealthy and aristocratic Briton, sojourning in the Land of Philistia and plenty on the 'other side,' are accustomed, and unless you can put up with seedy apparel, pipes, saucy female waiters who will be happy to share your breakfast, and the rather free and 'realistic' conversation of the quarter, principally consisting of medical and legal 'shop,' the fair sex, and the theatres, you had better stay on the 'other side,' and not intrude your spectacled nose into society incomprehensible to you, whose shibboleths are as hieroglyphics to you, and then write an article on the depravity of the French.

In one of these cafés, two men—not workmen this time—are sitting, eagerly conversing with one another. The purpose of this chapter is not, as the reader

supposes, to diffuse opinions on archi-
tectural and social reform, but to explain
who these two individuals are, why they
are there, and what they are talking about.
To effect this, we will, if you please, go
back half an hour or so into the earlier
part of this September morning, and enter
a studio on the fourth floor of an old house
in the Rue de la Harpe, on whose door is
nailed a visiting card :

'Paul Félix,
Artiste—Peintre.'

Through the studio, which is untidy, large,
and full of work mostly unfinished, we
will walk, and find ourselves in the bedroom (if your sense of propriety has not
already made you hesitate, not knowing
him as I do) of the said Paul Félix, and
behold him, in a shirt and a pair of
trousers, leisurely balancing on the side of
his bed, with a cigarette dangling lazily
from the corner of his mouth. The sun

shines fully and cruelly on the not un-
comely but worn face of a quite young man,
remorselessly displaying a complexion indi-
cative of late hours, and those habits
usually described by the vague euphemism
'irregular.' His hair is long, leonine and
curly, and deep red; a moustache feline
and bristly decorates his upper lip. His
cheeks and chin are, or rather soon will be,
shaved, his nose is aquiline, and his eyes
brown. The whole expression looks careless, sensible to humour, and unutterably
lazy, if you can imagine all that packed
into one expression. On a chair sits his
friend, Dr. Ivor Taylor, an American
Parisian, completely *enfant de Paris*, but
preserving always, throughout his fluent
French, inaccuracy of accent and grammar,
and his American straightforward, hit-and-
slash style of diction. His appearance is
as antithetic as possible to that of Félix.
He is perhaps a year older, but his dark

grizzled hair and the eternal Parisian moustache, also iron grey, wrinkled eyelids, and thin lantern-jawed face, not unhandsome withal, and a pair of spectacles, give him the air of at least ten years' seniority. His frame is strongly built, and he looks the personification of force, candour, and energy—something about him always suggesting a calm and courageous house-dog of massive proportions and gentle eyes. His close-cropped hair adds to the illusion. Their conversation was of course in French, but as this story is English, not French, it is advisable to translate it,

'Well, now that you have deprived me of hours of my well-deserved rest,' began the painter, 'what have you to tell me? Is there any news? or did you merely come to annoy me, by protruding before me the horrible regularity and industry of your life, as an example which you know I never can or will follow?'

' I haven't any news, except that it rained last night. I came to see you and ask how you were getting along.'

' Then I suppose all the news and conversation must come from me. Take a cigarette, and I will tell you a romance— such a one as your fog and filth beladen country never will or can produce.'

' I think you are mixing up my country with England. You evidently know little of either, so go on with the story—glad to hear some new thing.'

' Well, I have discovered a new *belle amie.*'

' Nothing new or surprising about that. Happens about once a week, don't it ?'

' —Whom you will not presume to make cumbrous American love to, or I will slay you. I fence better than you.'

' Better not show her to me, then.'

' But the whole glory and advantage of a *belle amie* consists in showing her, and boasting of her.

It is as if you had successfully coloured a meerschaum pipe. It is no satisfaction except to draw the envious admiration of your friends.

'All very well in pipes; not my notion to treat girls quite the same way.'

'Why not? They are very much alike —both pretty—both easily go to destruction, and both you get tired of when you have burned the beauty out of them!'

'Well, we won't discuss ethics. We shan't alter the eternal unfitness of things much, that way, I guess. Where's the story?'

'The story? Ah, yes. By the way your visit, you know, has charmed me in every respect, but it has not removed my appetite. Suppose we go and breakfast? The story will go better with a glass of wine and a cigarette, preceded by, we'll say, bread and butter, and perhaps cheese as you are with me—for which meal, and for this occasion only, I will permit you to pay, my own resources having an unusual strain upon them at this moment. Shall we go ?'

'Do you think of going as you are ?'

'Why not ? It is picturesque, and has a certain savage beauty about it, which it takes a true artist to appreciate.'

'I, not being a true artist, would press you to a little less picturesque, and a little more civilised, if I am going to walk out with you.'

'I sacrifice myself to prejudice and Philistinism. Come into the studio a minute. I have a surprise for you.'

Felix got up and strode from the bedroom to the studio, where he stooped over and appeared to unravel a kind of nest, composed mainly of blanket, and disclosed in this, in the seat of his own arm-chair, a minute, pallid, brown-eyed infant, of the female sex. 'You wanted to see my newly discovered *belle amie.* There she is !

Whether she can accommodate herself to an atmosphere of carbonate of lead, varnish, cognac and caporal tobacco, I know not. We are going to try.'

Dr. Taylor put on his glasses and inspected it minutely, as if it were a sea-anemone, or a cancer. It feebly and helplessly waved small tentacle-like limbs, and finally anchored its fingers in his grizzly black moustache, and hauled at it. 'Not the first of its sex that's done *that*, mon cher,' remarked the painter, laughing.

'Where in thunder did he get that?' exclaimed the bewildered American in his native tongue.

'Entirely my own opinion,' replied the other, in *his* native tongue.

'What's this?' asked Taylor, relapsing into French. 'A human being; young specimen; sex, female. Rare in this locality—at that age, at any rate.'

'Where did you get it?'

'That, my friend, is the story.'

Dr. Taylor gazed at it with an expression of gloom and embarrassment, and after some silence remarked :

'I suppose it's pretty ?'

'Pretty ? Good heavens, she's perfectly beautiful ! But it takes an artist's eye—mine, for example—to see that.'

'Doubtless. I don't know anything about that kind of being, except professionally.

'Except professionally. Of course, neither do I ; but then my profession leads me to study the outsides of beings, yours merely the insides ; which reminds me that our own insides require speedy replenishment. Therefore I will adorn myself ; I am about to shave. Now don't speak to me, or make me laugh, or bang the door, or stick pins into the infant, or anything calculated to make me cut my throat.'

Some moments passed ; after which Félix appeared in a rather ancient frock-coat, his hair combed, and on his head a tall hat, slightly on one side, and bearing an appearance of antiquity equal at least to that of the coat, and wearing round his neck a flowing crimson handkerchief, which toned down the rather conflagration-suggesting hue of his hair.

'How do I look now?' asked he, turning up his moustaches and striking an attitude.

'Just the same hopeless mixture of vagabond and baby that you always do ; come along.'

You, aristocratic Briton from the 'other side,' whom I have previously had the honour of apostrophising, had you seen Paul Félix, would have pronounced him a thorough cad. That only shows that you are too hasty in forming judgments from external appearances, and have not a suffi-

ciently wide acquaintance with mankind
to possess sympathy and largeness of
mind. For Paul Félix was nothing of
the sort; and could enjoy a Greek play
as much and more than an opéra bouffe,
and that is more than you can say.
Excuse plain language.

'Now we will go into the Boulevard, to
Madame Triboulet, and have coffee, and
ask Césarine's advice. I will take your
arm, as that seems to irritate you more
than anything else in public.'

As they walked along the pavement, in
the morning sunlight, Taylor said:

'Has it ever occurred to you to ask
yourself what is going to become of you?
What are you going to do? How are you
going to live? You can't keep up this
sort of existence for ever, you know.'

'I never speculate on such a very unsafe
and unpleasant subject as my future; and
no one but an outspoken old bear like

yourself would have wounded me by alluding to it. I am having an idle fit just now. I sometimes do.'

'I believe your last idle fit has lasted about three-and-twenty years.'

'Idleness is necessary to the artistic temperament.'

'Artistic *blague!*'

'Besides, I have not been idle. What was I to do! I came here, ostensibly, to study medicine—at least such was the intention of my guardians, who hoped that some day the Faculty, in a fit of temporary aberration of intellect, might make me a doctor. But dissections and operations had not the attraction for me they have for more fortunate and more utilitarian minds, and I devoted myself to human and mental physiology, giving my attention chiefly to its phenomena as manifested by the other sex—also to the consumption of the excellent beer and tobacco of the

Quarter. I hoped that by continually absenting myself from the Amphitheatre of Anatomy, I might learn to long for it —long separation is said to produce such longing. It apparently has not been long enough, as yet, though. Then, as you are perhaps not aware, my versatile genius longed for an outlet somewhere, and thought it had found it in journalism. I joined myself to two unwashed enthusiasts, who were pleased to style themselves editor and staff (I don't remember which took the part of the staff now), and wrote a *feuilleton* for their paper, the *Evening Bat.* This journal was started ostensibly to convince the inhabitants of Belleville of the fatal effects which a government, laws, and police must necessarily have on such a humanly perfect community as that of the Parisian working-class ; really, to provide a little bread and meat and cheap wine to the parties who

2—2

produced the journal.   My story was of a
nature calculated to wither to the marrow
and shake on their thrones all the crowned
heads of Europe—if they had only read it,
which they, in their blindness, failed to do.
I imitated Victor Hugo, and wrote in
short, possibly pithy sentences, and talked
about the giants and spectres of '93 on
every other page.   Here, however, the
resemblance ceased.   Victor Hugo did *not*
write to inform me that I was an
Apocalypse, though the sub-editor forged
a letter from him to that effect. Gambetta
did not give me the notice and patronage
due to my influence and sentiments.   The
crowned heads remained on their thrones,
and the paper fell through from lack of
support before the editor had time to
realise his pet ambition of getting im-
prisoned for sedition, which would have
sold the paper a thousand a day. A fine
would have been nothing to him. You

cannot fine a man who has no money. So I came to the conclusion that literature was not the path provided for me by the fates, and returned to my old study of human psychology, and here I am. I've got an idea——'

'You have got a tongue, anyhow. Now, suppose you listen to me. I am not moral and all that sort of thing, as you know, but I have certain sentiments, and prejudices as you will call them, and I've been in the world a trifle longer than you have, and I'll tell you this much. Paris is not the whole world, as you seem to think, and my sympathies spread beyond the Barrière de l'Etoile, even across the Atlantic, where I know certain old folks at home —not educated like us, though they had me educated; not looking at things the way we do, perhaps, but seeing the world through old-fashioned spectacles — have sent me here at their expense, with the money they've worked for and I haven't, to learn things, and come back from Europe a better and a wiser man. They think I'm working hard, and behaving proper, and going to church with a high hat on Sundays. Well, I can't go to church now. You and your modern thought and scepticism and progress and all that have taken away from me all that the old folks believe in; but I am entirely blasted if I don't do something—not much, but what I can—to come up to their expectations. No one ever does come up to his parents' expectations, but I guess I'm trying. How am I to account for my grey hairs and knowledge of the world to my mother? Just think of that. You know how one gets grey hairs here. You know what sort of a world one gets knowledge of here, and I confess I like that world. But you can enjoy life and work too. Now, just chuck off that cursed don't care, don't believe sort of tone you are putting on, and put yourself in the same position with regard to your relations, and honestly say if you ain't behaving like a d——d ungrateful young fool!'

'My dear sir, your words contain all the rude wisdom of the Bible, together with all the impracticable principles of that valuable work. You, in spite of your dissections and nasal accent, are a poet, minus the power of writing verse. I know you like sunsets, for you never go into eloquent rapture when you see one, but keep still. You also love humanity and revere women, in spite of your rather inconsistent behaviour to them. Now, with all this, it is perfectly natural that your sentiments should be what they are. I am not of the same constitution ; I do not feel any particular affection for humanity at large, and I believe the feeling is pretty mutual. As regards obligations to others,

I have no such embarrassments as expectant fathers and mothers; and the only relations I have, would say, with a sigh of relief, " I told you so !" if I were guillotined at three this afternoon. So that objection to my conduct falls to the ground. Your world may go beyond Paris. Mine does not. At least, not further than Asnières by steamboat on Sunday afternoons. My whole life is bound up with Paris. Have I never had any human feelings ? Good heavens, yes —but they have been cauterised out of me. Did you ever see the only girl you ever loved, when you believed in love, lying on a marble table in the Amphitheatre of Anatomy, with a score of students grinning at the exhibition through eyeglasses, and saying, " You knew her, Félix, didn't you ?" Now you can realise that I do not feel vehemently attracted towards that place. I don't respect

women. There is very little to respect about
them. They, like men, follow their desires
and feelings, and do not succeed in veiling
that fact so easily as men — that is the
only difference. The devil alone knows
what there is in your society that always
makes me serious and sentimental. Here
is our café ; come in, and change the
subject.'

Here they entered one of the above
alluded to brasseries, solitary at this early
hour, but destined to be filled later in the
day, and most of all later in the night,
with a jovial, laughing, reckless crowd of
students, and those flirting waitresses
who are such a characteristic of such
places, some of whom are attractive, all
of whom possess ready tongues and eyes
—and, I may add, ready appetites, and
an eternal thirst, and who make their
breakfasts, dinners and suppers, and sundry
interposed and miscellaneous courses of

refreshments, off the charity of their sworn friend, allies and protectors, the students.

Of these only one, Césarine, was present, fixing on an apron leisurely before a mirror, and rectifying the set of her hair, her mouth full of pins. Her Félix accosted :

'Césarine, thou of the classical name, wilt thou bring us certain portions of bread, butter, cheese, salt and wine—as usual? The only unusual element about the repast is, that it will be paid for, and that by our learned friend here.'

'What will you have yourself, Césarine?' asked Dr. Taylor.

Césarine confessed a longing for her favourite beverage, 'Vermouth gommé.'

Dr. Taylor said :

'Very bad for you so early. However, it is no use, I suppose, to tell you that. Bring it quick, with the other things— there's a dear.'

Césarine disappeared, and quickly re-appeared bearing a tray, whose contents, viz. the desired breakfast, she arranged at a table, and sat down with the two sons of Bohemia, and clinked glasses with them. Having eaten with the voracious appetite and unimpaired and omnipotent digestion of a schoolboy plunging for the first time into dissipation, Félix said:

'Now for the story. Listen to it, Césarine, and bear out the truth, if necessary, by your testimony.'

'That depends if there is any truth to bear out,' replied she, mindful of previous confidential revelations from the young painter.

'It is the privilege of your sex to be impertinent. Last night, near midnight, I was here, with the intention of enjoying Strasbourg beer and mademoiselle here's charming conversation. But seeing that she was already engrossed by other and doubtless more attractive friends——'

' Hear, hear !' from Césarine.

' I lit a cigarette, turned up the collar of my coat, and strolled out under the stars into the wide world, especially that portion of it bordering on the Seine. I paused under a lamp-post, ostensibly with the aim of looking at my watch, really to look at a remarkably pretty woman who was passing under the lamp at the same time. She carried a bundle, and wore one of those coffee-coloured mantles which forty thousand other women wear just now, and which consequently is no identification. She went on to the Pont St. Michel. So did I. She deposited the bundle on the pavement in the middle of the bridge. I looked at it. It was an infant. Of course I picked it up, overtook her, took off my hat, and observed : " Pardon, but madam has dropped something."

' She looked at me and it in some surprise, and replied : " Monsieur is exceedingly polite. As a consideration for his attention, I make over to his charge and protection that," pointing to the bundle.

' " May I inquire madame's name and address ?'

' " I regret that circumstances prevent my giving either the one or the other, and would suggest that I will trust to the sense of chivalry which monsieur has already shown he possesses, to prevent his following me further. Good-night."

' What was I to do? In your own poetic language, I vow, it was a " go." Figure to yourself me, alone and unprotected, in the middle of the night, in the clutches of a remorseless baby ! To drop it quietly over the parapet, and stroll away whistling as I passed the police, would have been convenient, but a crime—besides, these things are always found out. I put my hat forward, rounded my back, limped and tried to look as much like some one else as possible, in case any friend should find me in such compromising society, and put up an umbrella, although it was not raining, and got into the first cab I met and went home. The infant complicated matters by beginning to wail and lament. Now it is in my armchair, and will soon die of inanition if you don't tell me what I am to give it. I offered it brandy and beer, last night—excellent beer, but it rejected it with some violence. I ask your advice, as a friend, Césarine.'

Césarine, choking with laughter at the idea of a young bachelor of the Quartier 'raising' an infant on beer, said : 'Give it milk.'

'How much ?'

'Oh, as much as it will take, I suppose. I don't know.'

'Go and get some, will you ? You must come and see and criticise it, and display that mad and animal idolatry which all

young women have for the very young of
their species.' And the good-natured girl
disappeared, to inquire if such a fluid existed in the establishment. When she was
gone, Félix said :

'Now I have a proposition to make.
Don't be surprised or come out with ob-
jections till I have done. It is that you
and I, under the direction and advice of
Césarine, do undertake herewith and hence-
forward the up-bringing, physical and
moral, of the said female child, now residing in an armchair, fourth floor, No 25,
Rue de la Harpe, Quartier Latin, Paris.
Your medical knowledge will be occasionally useful. More than this. You know
what sort of life, and education, and morals,
girls in this quarter usually acquire. They
are like the flowers fallen from the jasmine
tree, that I saw at Asnières this autumn,
some still fair, and fresh and beautiful
lying there, some utterly withered and

destroyed, but with enough of the flower's soul and body about them to remind one that they were once beautiful jasmine blossoms, filling the summer with scent. Now I want to protect her, with your help, from all this. I want to carve out for her an ideal, artistic existence, untainted alike by the prejudices of the rigidly righteous or the foulness of the hopelessly fallen ; and I want you to enter into a bargain or contract with me, that whichever of us lives longest is to continue to care for and preserve our small jasmine flower, who promises to be pretty, and whom the fates have cast in our path. Will you do this ?'

'By the Lord in whom I don't believe, I will ! Shake hands, sir ; there's a man alive in your body yet.'

'We will give her a name : I will baptize her in champagne, which Madame Triboulet here will give on tick for such a charitable, not to say religious, purpose, and the provision for her future will be a stimulus to us to work hard, and a slight recompense to her sex for the many wrongs we have done them, and the many hard things we have said of them.'

Césarine here entered with a dark wine-bottle, through which came the greenish gleams of milk.

'Hum! doesn't look nice. No accounting for tastes,' commented Félix. 'You're a good fellow, Césarine; proud to know you — give me a kiss.' And he told her his plan with the eloquence of a sincere man, and casting aside his habitual tone of bantering flippancy.

Césarine was silent for a while, then said :

'I'll help where I can.'

She was thinking of her own life, though Félix purposely spared any allusions which might bring her lost past too prominently before this frivolous foam-born girl of the Quarter,

The whole undertaking was strange, original, and to an unimaginative mind impracticable. It was founded by two men, purely and solely out of their own instincts, uncontrolled by sense of duty, morality, or religion, and as such would surely be predicted to fail. Whether it did or not we shall see. Félix took Ivor Taylor's arm under his own on one side, and the black bottle under the other, and went away.

Césarine observed to old Madame Triboulet, the proprietress, who was engaged in the useful if prosaic occupation of peeling potatoes in an inner room :

'I think, M. Paul Félix is rather mad, but I like him all the same.'

CHAPTER II.

BAPTISM IN WINE AND FIRE.

THE baby discovered by Paul Félix came to have the name of Rosa. 'Rosa la Rose,' as Paul remarked, with a reminiscence of Latin grammar in his head. Surnames are not absolutely necessary commodities among the inhabitants of the Quartier Latin. They are often ignored, and do not always exist. This rule holds more particularly among the female portion of the community. So it was not thought necessary by Paul to invent one for his small charge.

She was baptized 'Rosa la Rose' by a

select company of Paul's most intimate friends in his studio, he himself of course officiating. He produced champagne and handed it round in glasses, accompanied by cigarettes. Césarine obtained a holiday, and was present. She took an immense interest in the child, and constituted herself *marraine.* Paul made a short speech, of course. No action was satisfactory or complete with him unless accompanied by a short speech. He explained his purpose with regard to the just then sleeping Rosa, and invited them all to co-operate and constitute themselves her guardians. They waved their glasses and exclaimed, 'Nous le jurons!'

The presence of the unconscious child seemed to recall everything that was pure, virtuous, past and gone and for ever out of their reach to the three or four reckless, billiard-playing, Bullier-frequenting young men present, and they really meant in all honour to be moral guardians to Rosa. Paul went on :

'I now baptize thee, Rosa la Rose, with the first foam of my wine, in hopes that you may grow to be like the glorious mother of gods and men who was born from the foam of the ocean. May your life be happy. I call you Rosa—

> ' " Parceque les plus belle choses,
> Comme les lis et les roses,
> N'ont qu'un saison d'été."

Vive Rosa, fille du Quartier Latin !'

'Vive Rosa, fille du Quartier Latin !' replied everyone, emptying his glass.

Rosa awoke. She looked round at all the strange faces with a stare of surprise.

'Oughtn't some one to kiss her ?' asked a student, whose acquaintance with the ancient and religious ceremony of baptism was somewhat rudimentary and vague in details.

'No man of us shall kiss her,' said Paul, 'until she can give him leave or signify her wish that he should do so. Césarine may, if she likes.'

'I had rather not,' said Césarine, rather sadly. 'I would like to. I am not more fit to kiss her than anyone here, simply because I am a woman and you are all men.' [She went and looked at Rosa, lying in the armchair of honour. Rosa knew best who was fit to kiss her, and stretched out her arms towards Césarine's neck and smiled. Césarine overcame all scruples, and embraced the baby Rosa in that greedy manner peculiar to women dealing with children or other animals of whom they are specially fond.] 'I wonder if you will show as much charity to one like me when you are older,' said Césarine, laughing.

'I think the godfathers, Taylor and myself,' said Paul, 'ought to kiss the

godmother as a natural part of the ceremony.

He saw Césarine was depressed and
saddened about something. It was possible to guess what, and wanted to change
the subject.

'I fail to see the doctrine of that,' said
the student, who had previously spoken,
who was not a godfather. Paul began
elaborately to argue the point, and
threatened to appeal to the Fathers, when
Césarine settled the matter by saying "au
revoir, messieurs !' and leaving the room.

'So Rosa has become Rosa,' remarked
Paul. 'Now the question remains, what in
the world is to become of her further ? Can
we control a destiny, or is she to control
ours ? It seems rather like the latter'
hitherto. Taylor, I shall depend on you
to assist in her education and amusement.
I will work—I have been promised a connection with a comic paper of importance

—and shall sell pictures, and work like a fever. On Sundays we will take her to the Luxembourg and the Tuileries.'

'Shall we buy a perambulator?' asked Dr. Taylor.

'I think not. You would look very well, though, disguised as a *bonne*. They often have moustaches.'

'We can bring her up to speak two languages,' said the other. 'You always speak French to her, and I will always speak American.'

This really happened. Rosa learned gradually both these languages.

Rosa gradually grew to the age of ten. Dr. Taylor postponed his return to America till he had heard her speak distinct and intelligible American, and then found himself obliged to leave. He and Paul took the child, then aged about eight, for their last excursion together to the Champs Elysées one Sunday afternoon. She rode in a carrousel. They rode too, merely of course to encourage her. In the interval between one of these rides, Taylor made the new and original observation :

'What an extraordinary couple we are !'

'We are,' replied Paul solemnly. He then added : 'But how is Rosa to keep up her American when you are gone ?'

'I don't know. Depends on luck. I will come and see her again some day. Look here, if any necessity arises, you send to me, will you ?'

'I will. You are Rosa's other god-father, and I believe she likes us both equally. I do not know what sort of a girl she will turn into, after our bringing her up. It seems to me inculcating moral principles is not our line. Her morality is our morality—that is, nothing particular. Her rules of life are ours, that one must do what one is compelled to do, and if one likes it, so much the better. When there is any choice, do what is pleasantest.'

'She is going to be pretty, too,' said Taylor.

Rose was small and dark, with a pale face and brown eyes. She looked as if she would be pretty, later.

'Well, my friend, we have done what we could. It may have been a Quixotic undertaking, and probably was; but it has made her happy, and, I think, has made us rather different. Fate and the future will do what they please.'

Dr. Ivor Taylor went home to the United States. Rosa sat on Paul's knee, and cried a good deal quietly, in the cab that brought them back from the railway-station.

She then became more than ever the attached friend of Paul. She had always loved him, and the studio, the pictures, and the armchair which had been given up to her ; but had an almost equal affection for Ivor Taylor, who had taken immense trouble to amuse and educate her in a fashion of his own, and took her to theatres, and cafés, and cirques, not perhaps the best selected entertainments for a young girl, but which certainly had the effect of giving her enjoyment.

This extra burden was handed over to Paul, who had now become staid and respectable and industrious, not of course from an ordinary point of view, but compared to his former and younger self. His adult life might indeed be divided into two epochs, that before and that after the discovery of Rosa. His pictures sold, and his studio was less of a den, and his furniture grew gradually more and more plentiful and comfortable. He rented a small bedroom for Rosa, and was in a fair way to become a rising young painter.

Rosa learned to eat chocolate and bon-

bons generally, and to regard them as the more serious and necessary ingredients of life. At the age of ten she smoked cigarettes.

At this period the happiness and tranquillity of Paris was rather marred by the advance of the German army upon that city, little as they believed, in Paris, in an ultimate German success. Still, annihilated as they were doubless destined to be by a patriotic nation rising *en masse* to defend its hearths and homes, the Prussians contrived in the meantime, during the winter of '70, to give Paris considerable embarrassment by surrounding it, taking its star-forts, and occasionally dropping shells into its suburbs, and, worst of all, cutting off its supplies.

All this was of course new and interesting to Rosa. Paul told her she was going to enjoy all the advantages of a real war, with real obuses, which really damaged bricks and mortar and imprudent human beings, and that it was all far superior, from an artistic standpoint, to the Battle of Solferino at the Circus.

Rosa quite fell in with this view, unaware that Paul sold half his portion of daily food to buy her chocolate, and rather enjoyed the siege, until one day, walking out for some purpose or other with Césarine, she saw some soldiers carrying a hideously mutilated mass, clothed in a torn uniform, into a church. This was the remains of a sentry who had been standing in the range of a shell battery, on the ramparts. This was the first real symptom of war Rosa had seen. She had heard guns in the distance, and knew that Paris looked rather different and more dull than usual, but on seeing the horrible reality of that wounded man, she woke up to a consciousness that war was not wholly picturesque.

Matters gradually grew worse. Instead

of the bright boy-like man that Paul the
painter had been, Rosa now saw a gaunt,
grizzly-bearded, sad-looking creature, who,
as Paul the National Guard, went peri-
odically to do sentry on snowy ramparts
under that unsympathetic starry winter
sky, which shines its brightest on human
sorrow and woe. He sat over the stove
in the studio, occasionally becoming jocular
in a spasmodic way when Rosa was present,
and smoked cigarettes when he could get
them. Rosa took this occasion, when
nourishment was so scarce, to grow a good
deal and become rather weak. She also
dreamed frequently that Paul would be
brought home like that wounded soldier,
some night from his post. The fact of
being a sentinel brought him home with a
renewed appetite, given him by the frosty
air. He once said : ‘ If I had known long
ago how easy it was to get a healthy
hunger in the morning, I should have tried

it before. I shall recommend a siege as an excellent remedy to persons suffering from dyspepsia and loss of appetite.'

So matters went on, week after week, until a catastrophe came.

A sortie was made from Paris: a very badly made sortie, one among many such, and an utterly ineffectual one. Paul Félix went out in it, and came back with a bullet in his chest. He was brought to a church full, like the rest, of wounded. Césarine was in some manner made aware of it, and came to fetch Rosa.

'What does he look like?' asked Rosa, shivering with terror; 'is he like that man we saw?'

'I don't know. He has a bullet in the chest. That ought not to show much.'

Rosa silently put on some clothes, to protect her from the cold, as if she were going out for a walk—a furred jacket Paul had given her, as he had given her most

other things—and went off with Césarine.
It was a long walk, and they did not speak
much by the way. They found the
church. At the door a sentry asked what
they wanted. Rosa spoke.

'We want to see Paul Félix ?'

A young doctor was talking to a Sister
of Charity in the doorway. He looked
round, and said :

'You can admit her, cntry : it is Rosa
la Rose. Paul Félix is her father.'

This was not true, but it served its
purpose, and Rosa and Césarine went in.

'You will find him at the other end,
near the altar, on the left-hand side. You
had better look neither to the right nor
to the left till you get there. Poor child !'
he added to himself.

It was one of the students who had been
present at Rosa's baptism. Rosa shut her
eyes and took Césarine's arm. The atmosphere of chloroform, carbolic acid, and other

miscellaneous ·and worse odours, confined
by want of ventilation, were sufficient to
bear, without seeing what lay to the right
and left of her. A well-known voice at
last came from the dark heap near the
altar, saying in a feeble tone :

'Rosa!'

Rosa saw the poor painter lying on his
back, with great hollow eyes, into which
the old gay smile came as he looked at her.
An overcoat was lying on his body. He
then said :

'The game is played out. So am I.
Césarine, you will write, or telegraph, as
soon as possible to Taylor, in New York,
and tell him all this. Are you warm
enough, Rosa, in that fur thing?

'"Car c'est l'étui d'une perle fine
La robe de Mimi Pinson."

Tell Taylor that is the last song I sang.
Tell him I am gone to meet Mürger, and
Musset, and Mimi, and Musette in such a

Quartier Latin as they may have in
Tartarus. Doctor says I am to die—
could not have done it better than now—
Listen ! I beg to correct myself, Césarine.
Tell Taylor *this* is the last song I sang——'
And the noise of a passing crowd of
soldiers, hurrying to the ramparts, was
heard shouting the memorable and formid-
able words :

> ' Aux armes, citoyens !
> Formez vos bataillons !'

Paul raised himself on both elbows, and
sang with a blaze of joy in his dark eyes :

> ' " Marchons, ça ira !
> Marchons, ça ira!
> Qu'un sang impur
> Abreuve nos sillons."'

And then the blood came up into his
mouth, and he fell back dead. Césarine
was crying quietly. Rosa was not. She
was very pale, and in a cold perspiration.
Césarine took her away. She fainted

when they got home, and then lay face
downwards on her bed and cried for a long
time.   And this was the end of Paul
Félix.

CHAPTER III.

EAVE LODGE, WINTERDALE.

'I want a hero ; an uncommon want
When every year and month sends forth a new one.'
BYRON.

IN a county in the south of England, the
name of which is immaterial—say Damp-
shire or Dirtshire—there is an antique little
town, once of historic importance, but now
almost completely insignificant from a public
point of view, called Winterdale. It con-
tains a gaol, a cathedral, a barrack, a bishop,
several minor canons, four churches, fourteen chapels, and at least forty public-
houses. The churches and chapels are full
on one day in the week, the public-houses
on six, the gaol on seven. The barrack is

never quite full, as it has to contribute to keep the other above-mentioned institutions filled, in varying proportions. The bishop is, or was when Winterdale became involved in this story, a tall, dignified man, of commanding and ascetic presence, and possessing a resonant voice. He gave garden-parties, and sermons and addresses; was bullied by his junior clergy, was very affable, and in every respect resembled any other commonplace bishop, and signed himself John James Hiemval. His real name was Green, but it is a customary piece of episcopal playfulness to name one's self after the diocese, translating the name of the latter into dubious Latin, which imposes on the unlettered (who constitute the majority of the population of any diocese), and would cause much honest mirth to any ancient Roman who might read it, and recognise the fine, old, widespread canine dialect to be found pervading ecclesiastic literature throughout all the years in which there was any church at all that had a literature.

The cathedral was mostly in the early perpendicular style, with a stumpy square tower in the middle.

The gaol was in the modern rectangular and utilitarian style, of black-brick walls, and apertures richly ornate with iron-work usually taking the form of bars and spikes.

The streets of Winterdale were quaint and irregular, and contained comfortable-looking inns of indefinite age, with court-yards and wooden or brick colonnades, under which persons might, and frequently did, sit round tables when the temperature permitted. When some of the soldiers continually being localised in Winterdale were seen standing about and swaggering with boots and whips in the doorways, or gathered round beer in the verandas of these old inns, they had an exceedingly characteristic and picturesque appearance. The beer and other entertainment there provided was usually very good, so much as to be rather celebrated in the county.

On Saturday afternoon, when a market was held, the streets and alehouses became especially lively, and every lane was full of yokels and soldiers striving their rather feeble best to 'keep in de middle ob de road,' by closing-time on Saturday evenings. There was on such occasions plenty of the honest home-brewed ale floating about that the old school of novelists affect so much, and plenty of honest home-brewed headache and biliousness with it, assisted by the more deleterious and less honest spirits, which are theoretically manufactured in Nantes or Holland by the unscrupulous foreigner, which the British publican is too honest to manufacture, and can conscientiously only permit himself to sell, and that at a considerable profit. All the features of fine old English life, which have passed away in many places to such a lamentable extent, were to be found here. The countrymen wore smock-frocks, discarded elsewhere save by men who pick pockets in Fleet Street, and the associate of the thimble-rigger and the stage.

They observed with superstitious reverence and wonderful saturnalia the great Christian and Protestant festival of what they called 'Guyfox-day,' and the less important and pagan one of Yule-tide. They had holidays, made a hideous din with all the available church-bells, burned fires; cheered and sang, and eat and drank far too much on both of these occasions. Their idea of outward and visible manifestation of joy or religious exaltation took the form of excessive eating and drinking.

These were their religious festivals; referring of course to that portion of the

population which patronised the market
and the alehouse. The other and minor
portion of Winterdale society, consisting of
the clergy, military (active and retired),
and gentry, might observe harvest thanks-
givings and such things if they liked, which
the bulk of the rural population did not
'hold with.' They felt that the harvest
was entirely a merit of their own, to be
grumbled at if bad, and sold as dear as
possible if good, and failed to see what was
the use of the clergy and gentry coating
the churches internally with corn enough
to make a rick, and grapes, and apples, and
potatoes, and such other fruits as the season
yielded, and then holding services in the
midst of all this profusion, which were
attended by everyone except those interested and concerned in the production of a
harvest. They scornfully tolerated such
things, and observed, perhaps in lofty in-
dignation : 'If passon don't know no better

what to do with the carn and that, than to
make a litter and dirty mess with it in t'
church, he can give 'em to me.'

Society at Winterdale, as has been
hinted, consisted of the clergy, a few retired officers with families, and some
scattered country gentlemen whose profession in the main was to own land, chase
vermin with horses and dogs, and fill
'chairs' at sessions, and meetings of
Guardians, and Local Boards, and such
like distinguished and intelligent bodies,
and to give each other large dinner-parties.

The younger portion of society, the
tennis - playing, dancing, flirting portion,
consisted entirely and almost exclusively
of curates and young officers, and those
who hoped to be curates or young officers
some day, with very few exceptions. The
difference between the curates and the
officers was not great, consisting mainly in
the difference of uniform, and of the fact

that the lieutenants flirted and didn't marry, and the curates married and didn't flirt. At any rate so it appeared. It is difficult to say which were of the most use to the community, for both were of so little. Both were conceited, both were ignorant and opinionated, and constantly had to be 'sat upon' by their superiors, and both dressed very conspicuously. Here, however, the followers of Mars had the advantage. They came with their men to the cathedral on Sunday in full uniform, and although the curates came too, and bedecked and bedraped themselves with every wonderful and fearful bedizenment that folly can devise or conceit wear, ten pair of female eyes went to the military figures, motionless, upright and brilliant, to one that sought those of the curates.

The old retired officers, of both arms of the service, and the older clergy, were, in the main, foolish young ones grown up, and overpowered with the consequence of themselves and their opinions. There was a club at Winterdale, where the local gentry met, and talked long, eagerly and fiercely about nothing, for hours ; or, a less innocent amusement, dissected their neighbour's characters and financial uprightness, and circulated with the most innocent and sincere intentions most fearful and atrocious lies, which no one was responsible for, which did perhaps some little harm, but did not usually obtain any notice or credit.

The most entertaining and intelligent man actually in Winterdale was old Mr. Andrew McSwiney, M.D. (T.C.D.), the 'Doctor.' He was a short, sturdy man of the globular type, had a burnt, weather-beaten face like a coastguard, and a bald head, and a fringe of iron-grey hair round it. He was the life and soul of any entertainment or conversation. To ladies

he was kind and polite; and with the men
he could relate stories over tobacco and
Kinahan's L.L., till they nearly choked
with laughter. He never got drunk, but
could calmly absorb wine and spirits like a
large round sponge, or like any of Mr.
Charles Lever's Irish country gentlemen.
He was very kind and charitable, rather
impulsive, but withal possessed of great
acuteness and self-reliance; was no re-
specter of persons, feared not Dean or
Devil or Disease, and was universally
abused, laughed at, and loved.

About a mile outside Winterdale city,
among the rising downs and undulating
meadow and woodland, in the district of
St. Wotan, was an old country house,
called Eave Lodge, of lichenous grey lime-
stone, patched in many places with ivy,
and roofed with thin slabs of shaly
stone.

The date of the house was uncertain,

likewise the style of architecture. It stood on a piece of grass-ground which rose eastward, where the wind came from, into a small down, and westward stretched level, with irregularly placed trees and shrubs till it developed into a group of fir trees, on a slight eminence, which sent their stiff, slender spires and branches straight athwart the sunsets.

A path, paved accidentally with brown needles and fir-cones, led under these over-arching firs to an old wooden five-barred gate, covered with worm-tracks and snail-trails, with names encarven by the knife of youth, and softened and beautified by the lichen of age. A person leaning on this gate could see undulating, corn-pro-ducing country extending far to the west, and ending in cloudy woods on the distant horizon.

The grass grew right up to the walls of the house, and except for one square patch

of shaven lawn, intersected by a mystic
pattern of white-washed lines for lawn-
tennis, was allowed to grow freely and
long away under the yews and cypresses.
Yellow irises, tall lilies, and thistles and
sunflowers, and the miscellaneous herbage
known generally to gardeners as ' weeds,'
grew in the grass, under the trees, and
fringing this square lawn, in their seasons.
There was also on one side of the house
an old rose-garden with grass walks and
wooden seats, and beyond it an old apple-
orchard.

The house was fortified on the north-
west corner by a stone terrace, extending
round portions of the western and northern
side, on to which French windows opened
from the house. On its walls and parapet
hung heavy, rich clusters of jasmine,
clematis, and passion-flower. Theoretically
this terrace was destined by the architect,
no doubt, to be walked on when the grass

was too wet. As a matter of fact, the grass was usually the first to dry after rain, since the old stone pavement was hollowed, separated and broken into a series of receptacles for puddles, only to be removed by the beneficent natural law of evaporation.

Just now, September, 1871, autumn was beginning to make itself very apparent around Eave Lodge. This was an annual occurrence, although from the seemingly surprised and unprepared state of the neighbourhood, one might be led to suppose that such was not the case.

Old Diggory, who was called the gardener here, and who condescended to accept wages for occasionally visiting and severely criticising, spade in hand, the garden, if it might be so called, remarked sententiously that the 'days was gettin' in,' by which mysterious announcement he doubtless imagined himself to be conveying information of a new and useful description. He also delicately referred to the advent of rheumatism in what he was pleased to term his ' lines,' and person generally ; and admitted, on cross-exami-nation, that port-wine, or even rum (for strictly external application), would not be wholly unacceptable as a remedy.

The deciduous trees were becoming bronze, and the evergreens looked greener in contrast. The sun set gradually more to the southward of west. The mornings began with a chill mist, developing into a calm cool fine day, ending in a shower and a sunset behind scattered, ragged-edged black clouds, with glimpses of golden, red, and peach-coloured light at their under-edges, or through wind-torn holes, on a ground of white sky, becoming pale blue towards the zenith. Or else, perhaps, it blew hard, and acorns and leaves descended in heaps, and the heaven became grey and overcast, the wind south-east, and the temper of the fraction of humanity subjected to such weather deteriorated.

The fire-places, filled during the summer months with that truly awful form of decoration in which housemaids appear to delight, made of strips of paper of various colours and tinsel, became brilliant and inviting with burning coal and wood ; and it became almost comforting, as the weeks wore on, to read descriptions of disastrous fires in the papers, ascents of Mount Vesuvius, and sermons on eternal punishment.

Having so far touched on the external appearance and surroundings of Eave Lodge and its neighbourhood, it will now perhaps be as well to examine the internal or soul-part of the house, and the aspect of its inhabitants. It will be favourable to do so, and will give a characteristic view of these, by glancing at the drawing-room at five-o'clock tea-time on a Sunday after-noon in this autumn of 1871.

It is the room that opens by French windows (these framed with roses) on to the terrace—a long, rectangular, low room, with pale yellow walls, a high carven mantelpiece, supporting multitudinous china of many shapes and colours, and doubtless of incalculable age, pourtraying—

> 'Tales undoubtedly true
> In the reign of the Emperor Hwang,'

and furnishing capital lurking-places for dust and leaves and deceased spiders to get brushed together into heaps in by careful housemaids.

Various pictures, mostly modern and a little above the average of quality, and a few really charming etchings were on the walls. There was a piano in one corner. The furniture was dark-looking, of modern manufacture, and expressed comfort rather than any rigid adherence to high-art dictation. Little tables stood around, bearing the materials for afternoon-tea, which was administered in charmingly minute china cups, always a cause of trembling to the nervous visitor, unwilling to destroy his neighbours' goods.

Brackets and shelves in corners bore various useful and ornamental objects, such as brass candlesticks with ecclesiastical-looking, twisted stems, and cup-shaped upper extremities with scalloped edges; also bronze figures, flower-vases, Pompeian lamps, match-holders; and lastly, a clock, of some dark, polished and heavy-looking material, apparently of mineral origin, so constructed as to give the public a painful, if not indecent, insight into its throbbing vital organs—a sort of Alexis St. Martin among clocks.

Of course, a few 'library' books were

lying about, together with the *Contem-porary Review, Punch,* and the *Illustrated London News.*

Now let us glance at the occupants of this room in detail. There was, first of all, in an arm-chair on one side of the fire-place, an elderly gentleman of spare frame and strikingly intelligent appearance, and having rather long grey hair, grizzled brown whiskers clipped short, a long face, aquiline nose, bright blue eyes and rough grey-brown eyebrows, and a rather wide, thin-lipped mouth, with the wrinkles pro-duced by frequent speech and laughter at the corners, and a prominent, gracefully shaped chin and lower maxillary bone. This was Professor John Miller, the owner of the house, a great comparative ana-tomist, and recently retired from a pro-fessorship he had for some years held in the medical faculty of a celebrated and ancient Scotch university. He occupied himself in writing treatises for the scientific periodicals, and in enjoying the society of his family. A man of great general attainments, Scotch, kind-hearted, humorous, carelessly good-natured, and afraid of no man's opinion or of anything else. He was regarded as a man of some consequence by the scientific world, as a genius by his family, and as a kind of harmless lunatic by the majority of Winterdale society.

Conversing with him on a paper on Evolution in the review that lay between them on a table, sat a man of near his own age, tall, portly, bald, with regular features, long expressive dark eyes, and a long black beard. He was laying down the law with that decision peculiar to people imperfectly acquainted with their subject. This was Mr. James Exeter, vicar of the new parish of St. Wotan.

He and Professor Miller had been fellow-students at an English university together. They were so very antithetic in their tastes, opinions, and pursuits that they became fast friends.

James Exeter in those days pronounced John Miller to be a loose freethinker, though a pleasant enough fellow and clever in his way.

John Miller spoke of James Exeter as a good fellow, and clever in his way and well-read, though extraordinarily superstitious, and impervious to a joke.

James Exeter learned Hebrew and other ancient tongues, and became acquainted intimately with the Fathers, the Talmud, and the Septuagint, and studied decorative religious art, and crawled about the floors of old churches with a long sheet of paper, taking impressions of brasses ; and grew into a country vicar of apostolic and picturesque appearance.

John Miller plunged into acids and dissections and German poets and philosophers all at once, drank beer, sat up all night smoking clay pipes and singing songs with kindred spirits, made love to every available pretty girl, and grew into a retired professor, rather invalided, but with the fire of intellect burning fierce in his grey head, and keen and kindly fun glancing out of his Scotch blue eyes.

He had married an English lady, who was now present, a handsome old lady with white hair and black eyebrows, conversing with her sister the Marquise de Tortoleone, who had married a Frenchman, and was very French indeed, even to her accent, in consequence, and was as young, beautiful, and fashionable as human efforts could make her, though only a few years younger in reality than Mrs. Miller. She had been staying in England lately, in consequence of the war of the Commune in Paris. Her son, a regular-featured, dark, expressionless lad of fifteen was silently devouring currant-cake in a corner.

Professor Miller had a son, now aged eighteen—a handsome, fair, slender youth, with his father's long face and blue eyes and determined jaw, and his mother's straight nose—who just now was lounging against the mantelpiece with a cup of tea in his hand, and gazing through the window at the sunset. He was just at the end of his school career, and had been a pupil of Mr. Exeter's for some little time, with the aim of going in the ensuing October to the university.

It is worth while to look carefully at this youth with the far-gazing eyes, the short yellow hair, and the invisible moustache which he nervously feels for, for he, if any, is the hero of this story.

His sister, one year younger than himself, was occupied in the practice, which since the publication of 'Werther' has become memorable, of cutting thin slices of brown bread and butter. She was a pretty girl, with light-brown hair plaited into a tail, with the dignified air of one who imagines herself grown up, having just got past the uninteresting stage of girlhood and arrived at that physical change late, as is usual in fair persons, which produces all that natural development in a girl which changes her from an uninteresting and ungraceful nonentity to a very interesting and graceful entity. She was a good-natured, rather lazy girl, brought up at home, very properly and religiously, under her mother's eye, as any girl in early life ought to be, and instructed tolerably in the French and German languages—not in the Stratford-atte-Bow style, but by natives and visits to the various countries — also in music and ordinary drawing. She was generally liked, and few ventured to say a word

against her, as yet, even in Winterdale.

When Professor Miller's children were
born, he was strongly inclined to endow
them with scientific names, and threatened
to have them christened Epiphysis and
Diaphysis, or Incus and Mallea, or Auri-
cula and Ventriculus ; but these and their
like encountered such violent feminine
opposition that he was fain to let them
be named, after their parents, John and
Helen ; the boy being invariably known as
Jack to the world ; Helen the Professor
affectionately addressing always by the first
syllable of her name, at first, it is believed,
with the motive of shocking the vicar of
Winterdale, so that it ultimately became
a recognised practice and attracted no
attention.

Mr. Exeter was an object of great admiration and esteem to Mrs. Miller and
Hel. First of all, because he was 'papa's

old friend ;' and then because both their heads were replete with that earnest tragi-comic muddle of noble aspirations and formal trivialities which it pleases some ladies to term religion, and Mr. Exeter was just the man to encourage them. He was picturesque and grandiloquent in the pulpit, and his services were consummately supreme. Do not let it be supposed from this that Mrs. Miller was a fool. *Gott bewahre!* She was an estimable lady of more than average abilities, but, as her son respectfully remarked, ' Her one loose slate is religion, alias High Churchism.'

Mr. Exeter was not married. He had believed in the celibacy of the clergy ever since a young lady, an object of particular admiration to him in his curate days, had cruelly thrown him over in favour of a tall gentleman with very short hair, a very long, very drooping, and very ' silky ' moustache (*vide* feminine romance of the day, *passim*), large stand-up collars, and an uncontrollable habit of saying 'By Jove !' whose profession was to defend his country, or attack some one else's if ordered by his sovereign. Mr. Exeter, by an exquisite cruelty of the Parcæ, had been asked to assist in joining these two together at St. George's, Hanover Square, a labour which one clergyman appeared insufficient to perform. He had still a vivid recollection of hearing the bridegroom mutter an audible 'By Jove!' when he (James Exeter) pronounced in due course 'that these two be man and wife together.'

If Mr. Exeter had perused the maxims of the impious but amusing M. de la Rochefoucauld, he would have discovered another reason why he remained celibate : 'If we resist our passions it is because they are weak, rather than because we are strong.'

It is apparently a law of nature that disappointed lovers should take to dissipation of some form, sometimes of more than one form, as a temporary relief to the feeling. Some choose 'Our Lady of Pain,' others brandy, both more or less rapid forms of moral suicide if persisted in. James Exeter plunged into the fiercest excesses of Anglo-Catholicism.

His mind and time were now pretty fully occupied with services, sermons, Sunday - schools, and sundry such like forms of duty, and he had withal the consoling conviction that his time was being usefully as well as pleasantly spent.

He had found some of his parishioners largely prepared to assist in the practical carrying out of his views, as any enthusiastic good-looking man will find supporters, particularly among the females of a community, if even to get up a Guild for the Propagation of 'Hymns Ancient and

Modern' in the Moon. So Mrs. and Miss
Miller taught in the Sunday-school, of
which the little boys and girls of the parish
were the victims. The said Sunday-
school, by dint of illustrated 'tickets,'
treats, teas, buns, bunting, bands, and pro-
cessions, and sermons 'plain for children'
(and coloured for adults, added the flippant)
became well attended, to the intense
gratitude of the parents who got rid in this
way of their noisy and rowdy offspring for
a fraction of the day.

The Vicar also played cricket, without
being in the least a 'muscular Christian,'
though decidedly muscular and undeniably
a Christian. This endeared him to the
older lads of the parish, who respected him
far more because he could bowl them out
than because he was—according to his
pulpit assertions — a successor of the
apostles.

Finding Professor Miller apparently too

lazy this afternoon to contradict him on
Huxley and Darwin, Mr. Exeter adapted
his conversation to the supposed scale of
intelligence of a female audience, and
inquired if Miss Miller were going to the
Bishop's garden-party. Miss Miller hoped
so, but was not sure ; it depended on how
mamma was. 'Would Mr. Exeter have
another cup of tea ?'

'Thank you, if you please ; half a cup
will be plenty. Yes ; I was going to say,
Miss Miller, that you must persuade your
mamma to abstain from all risks of ail-
ments till then. I should be sorry for
you to miss it. The Bishop is to give an
address.'

'And when it is over and my duty
as chaperon done,' said Mrs. Miller, 'I
suppose I am at liberty to relapse again
into neuralgia and quietude to my heart's
content ?'

'I believe,' said Jack, 'Hel never

discovered that parents were of any use in life till just now, when she is always wanting chaperons.'

The Professor's quick Scotch tones were heard retorting :

' And you, Jack, have not found a use for us at all yet, except the one that occurred to you in earliest infancy, that we were a ready source of cash. Just think, Exeter, he began by soliciting pence to buy bull's-eyes and chocolate, on the ingenious pretext that they were for Hel or a beggar, or some equally deserving person, just to take away any lurking suspicion of greed on his own part, which of course had never entered our heads. Then he grew older, and required shillings for materials wherewith to compound fireworks and for other eminently scientific purposes. Six months ago he became ambitious to ride a bicycle, and having surreptitiously obtained one, permitted the bill to fall into my hands. I admit, with some pleasure, that he suffered a good deal in learning to ride it, and has not succeeded in destroying the instrument yet. He has recently discovered that colouring, and incidentally breaking, clay pipes is a manly and desirable accomplishment ; and I have reason to suppose has undergone much private anguish in acquiring it. It is a cheap amusement, however——'

'I say, draw it mild, father,' said Jack, laughing. 'You can't invent many more examples of extortion.'

'I do not think,' said Mr. Exeter gravely and pleadingly, 'that your son is quite so mercenary as you seem to think.'

Mr. Exeter wonders to this day why both Jack and his father laughed so much at this reply.

'We were just discussing when you came in, Exeter,' continued the Professor, in a different tone, 'what to do with this long youth—what profession he ought to adorn.'

' What profession do you feel inclined to, Jack ?' said Mr. Exeter.

' I'm not exactly sure. I might try medicine. I rather like the idea. What I really would like best would be to be an artist.'

' I think he had better study the pre-liminaries of medicine at Oxbridge,' said the Professor. ' He will learn a great deal there that is useful to know; and if he is to be a painter, the knowledge so obtained will be useful all the same. He wants to have some proper scientific train-ing, and to see how people really work at these things, instead of solitary dabblings in hand-books and water-colours. After Oxbridge, it is my wish and his own, whatever be his subsequent profession, that he should go to Paris.'

' The best thing he can do, Professor !'

exclaimed the Marquise, who had been hitherto rather silent.

'Do you really think so, madam?' inquired the Vicar, with some hesitation. 'Do you not think that would be leading a young man into many and unnecessary temptations?'

'Perhaps; but it would give him the best education in medicine or in art, and civilise him. I do not know what English universities are like, but imagine they must be rather—' barbarous, she was about to say, had she not suddenly recollected that the Professor, and probably his friend, were English university men, and so modified her termination to 'different,' which was rather weak.

'Ah!' said the Vicar; 'I often wish for my three years at the dear old college over again. You know, madam' (he was dubious how to address a marquise, and 'fluked' along), 'Professor Miller and my-

self were fellow-students at Oxbridge, and
we, or at any rate I, have the pardonable
opinion that in an English university is
found the best intellectual and social
education for a young man.'

'Yes; and a moral one,' added the
Professor. 'I found it so; didn't I,
Exeter?'

The Vicar smiled faintly, and shook his
head reprovingly.

'I did contemplate sending him to
Leipzig and Berlin, where I was myself
once; but I incline to Paris now, and so
does he. It is always well to study in a
European as well as an English or Scotch
university. It tends to remove the too
prevalent impression of the immeasurable
superiority of Great Britain in matters
social and intellectual.'

'Besides,' said the Marquise, 'in Paris
I can keep an eye on him.'

'Two, if you like,' replied the Professor,

'though I fancy by that time it will be considered immaterial by him whose eye is fixed on him.'

'Not altogether, I hope,' said Mrs. Miller gravely.

'Hadn't I better leave the room,' interposed Jack, with the delightful pertness of an only son, 'if you are all going to spend the afternoon talking about me?'

'If there is any painting in him,' said the Professor, 'it will break out of its own accord, and in the meantime a little general scientific education—on the top of your Æschylus and Horace, Exeter—will be no disadvantage, and may be even an assistance in other professions than medicine. Anatomy now, for example——'

Here the Marquise hastily changed the conversation, well aware what was likely to follow if her terrible and scientific brother-in-law once got the conversational bit in his teeth on anatomy, by asking:

'Do you have a musical service here, Mr. Exeter? You know I am a Catholic, but I take a great interest in these matters' ('She didn't the least, half-an-hour ago,' muttered the snubbed Professor), 'and would be happy to give any assistance I could.'

'Certainly. We do what we can with our little choir. There is nothing we should welcome so much as a lady's voice in the singing. You, perhaps, would be unaccustomed partly to our music and style of chant, but that would come readily after a few practices. We have a full choral service twice on Sundays, and an incompletely choral matins every week-day at 8 a.m. Besides which, we have, of course, the frequent occasional festivals, with which you must be as well acquainted as we, to enlighten the comparatively monotonous week, as well as the weddings and funerals. Ah, what a lovely funeral was that last

Thursday! I fancy you were not there, Miller?'

'I fancy not, Exeter. I have given up assisting professionally at parish death-beds now. Probably the next funeral I personally attend will be my own. Good that! Personally conducted funerals! Might advertise an agency for them, *à la* Cook.'

'You are incorrigibly flippant, Professor. May I ask,' proceeded Mr. Exeter to the Marquise, 'if we may expect you in our little church to-morrow—Sunday? The Bishop will preach, and it will be rather a favourable occasion for gaining a first impression.'

'Oh, certainly—thank you very much,' replied the Marquise, as if accepting an invitation to dinner. 'I have no doubt my sister will have great pleasure in taking me there.'

Hel and Jack were now sitting on a

sofa, displaying their discretion by talking about their visitor, as was perfectly obvious from their low and cautious tones and furtive glances at the object of their discourse. Mr. Exeter startled them by asking, during a lull in the conversation, if Miss Helen would not favour him with a song, and made remarks about Ulysses and the sirens, intending, of course, to institute a comparison between Miss Miller and a siren, it following naturally that he represented the subtle and travelled Greek.

'But I hope you are not going to stop your ears, Mr. Exeter,' replied Hel.

'I think I am right in saying that Ulysses stopped the ears of his crew and kept his own open. I shall follow his example and dispense with a crew.'

'Of course, Hel! Wrong again, as usual,' remarked Jack with masculine decision, calculated to display the superiority of the British boy's acquaintance with the ancient literature of Greece over that of the British girl.

Hel darted a fiery glance at her brother, and observed gravely, ' I am forgetting my Homer dreadfully,' as if Bentley, Wolff, Gladstone, and the inevitable Scholiast were her intimate friends, and with the satisfied tone of one who could readily tell you the shades of difference between two ἀυταρ ἐπει's in two consecutive sentences. As a matter of fact, she had once opened Pope's ' Homer's Iliad ' in the course of her existence, and in five minutes pronounced it heavy and stupid—to which opinion, as she journeys through life, she will find many adherents.

Hel arranged herself before the piano. Her particular enthusiasm just then was Germany, so she gave in a clear, expressive, though not powerful soprano, a German song—a common song enough, but beautiful when heard seldom. This

was Uhland's 'Es zogen drei Burschen
wohl ueber den Rhein,' telling how the
three students went in one after the other
to gaze on the body of the poor dead girl,
the 'Wirthin's Töchterlein,' and how the
first said he had loved her many a year;
the second that if she were not dead, he
would begin loving her from that day;
while the third went up to the bier, and
kissed her cold pale mouth, and said :

'Dich liebte ich immer, Dich lieb' ich noch Heut',
Dich werd' ich lieben in Ewigkeit.'

CHAPTER IV.

JACK MILLER.

'No, no; I'd send him out betimes to college,
    For there it was I picked up my own knowledge.'
                                        BYRON.

IT is now time to devote a few special words to our young friend Jack Miller, who will be a figure of some importance in these pages.

He was sent to school at the age of nine, where he remained till he was sixteen. It does not much signify which school; they are much alike. We will call it Whippingham. But Jack was not constructed quite after the pattern of all English schoolboys. He worked with facility, and spent his spare time in helping his friends. Of active games he was not over-fond. He preferred loafing in summer with a novel, to playing cricket. Cricket meant fielding to him, as he was a sorry batsman and could not bowl. In winter he occasionally played football with valour and violence, but without attaining much skill.

He read a Waverley novel at the age of nine, mispronouncing half the names, and gaining a somewhat hazy conception as to the meaning and point of some of the action; but, nevertheless, extracting a good deal of entertainment to himself therefrom. He organised bands of outlaws among the lower boys, who assembled at the sound of a whistle from the leafy glades of Sherwood (Sherwood consisting of a clump of laurels). He besieged Torquilstone, and repulsed the captors of Rob Roy with hard fallen chestnuts—one of

which nearly put another boy's eye out—and
so forth, until the dramatic representation
of the Waverley novels was summarily
prohibited, Dirk Hatteraick having surreptitiously procured a real pistol and shot
one of his invaders in the left hand.

At the age of twelve he read some
Tennyson, and pronounced it stupid and
affected—an opinion he had heard some
one else enounce. At seventeen he thought
it beautiful, and was constantly discovering
imaginary 'Mauds' in the most common-
place people twice his age.

Shakespeare he found an unfathomable
mine of delight. He had a great deal of miscellaneous literature at his hand at home.

He read popular science, and messed
with nitric acid and fireworks. He pur-
chased a small work on logic, at the insti-
gation of nobody, when he was fifteen;
and what is more, read it.

He found his father's collection of

books on anatomy (especially the morbid
branch), and on disease, and surgery, ex-
tremely interesting, and read them here
and there in a patchy style, and gave himself credit for knowing a good deal more
than he really did. Examinations took
that out of him in later life. He was very
fond of novels. At school he preferred
the sensational and incidental style, as represented by 'trappers,' redskins, Mexicans
who said ' Car-ramba !' and gentlemen who
rode about with their heads under their
arms. Later on, he became more fastidious,
and demanded a clever and bold style in
which ideas ranked above incidents. As a
boy, he wrote plays, of which the plots
were a result of accident rather than
design, and seldom arrived at a definite
dénouement. He had given that up.

Professor Mills had said :

' Jack, you can't write plays. Your
dramatis personæ are a fortuitous con-

course of actors from the novels you have read, and your blank verse is decidedly inferior to that of Shakespeare, whatever you may think to the contrary. You *can* draw, and you can work at science. Don't have too many irons in the fire, and don't be too sure of anything.'

Jack, temporarily annihilated, and wrathful, saw in time that there was sense and truth in his father's words, and ceased to be a dramatic author. He went, however, to the Winterdale School of Art, where he worked hard, made many friends, and acquired what skill in manipulation the place could give him, which, *plus* his natural talent, gave him a respectable power of representation.

At sixteen or seventeen he left school, and became a pupil of Mr. Exeter, residing of course at home. Naturally, his mind was not what is usually understood by pure, innocent, and moral. No one except

his mother could believe that an English
schoolboy of seven years' standing could be
all or any of these. If a proved specimen
is to be found, I should like to see it. He
had a certain code of ethics, such as never
to tell a lie except to shield a friend, or on
such like urgent necessity; never to hurt
other people if avoidable without loss of
prestige. He was with difficulty provoked,
and took most things pretty calmly. He
was not shy—

'C'était là son moindre defaut.'

But he could not be called forward or ill-
mannered, and was seldom impertinent.
He had a strong sense of justice, and
logic and Euclid combined to give him a
very clear insight into arguments. Reverence he was almost absolutely devoid of,
though he might admire and respect certain
persons and things.

Religion had been represented to him

at home, as well as at school, as a matter of authority, a foregone conclusion, a matter of course. His father had decided not to dictate to him in favour of, or against, distinct articles of belief, meaning to assist him when old enough to come to rational conclusions by using his own judgment. His mother had, of course, decided nothing of the kind, and instructed him, contemporaneously with his A B C, on the Bible and religion of the Church as matters to be believed, staggered and horrified as she might be by his occasional naïve matter-of-fact questions. All the preachers he had ever heard had done the same.

But at sixteen, logic, Euclid, curiosity and a strong bias for fact had set the stone of free thought rolling in Jack's active brain, and authority in matters of opinion and foregone conclusions sank and were shattered beneath it. His mind at first got into a quasi-religious, quasi-sceptical muddle. He endeavoured to worry out evidence, and think for himself. The result was that articles of faith became more and more pulverised, until the question came, Why believe at all? Know, or confess ignorance and absence of proof. And faith went overboard after its component parts. The result was, that Jack Miller at eighteen put on a tall hat and went to church, purely because he knew it pleased his mother that he should do so. She had prayed always that he might be an effective minister of the church. It caused her great grief to be so disappointed. This Jack was sorry for, but could not of course help, and restrained himself from pointing the case out as an example of the efficacy of prayer.

His character was pretty fully developed. Like many only sons of solitary habits and a fondness for reading, he had grown up a little too early. His tastes were not yet fully developed. He had been acquainted with many intelligent persons, among whom perhaps the most important was his own father, and was capable of sustaining a conversation with spirit and sense. He could speak and read French and German moderately well. It may be further added, for the benefit of the curious, that his hair was short, yellow, and parted in the middle ; his eyebrows not white, as everyone feared they would ; that he was five feet ten inches high, well shaped, though slender, and fond of bird's-eye. He could draw and colour well. At school he had covered his books with devices and designs, to the great ire of his masters. All schoolboys convert their books into repositories for superfluous ink, but few can draw beyond, perhaps, a rude representation of a human figure depending stiffly from a gibbet, with the inscription, 'This is old So-and-so.'

In the year 1870, the Emperor of the French endeavoured to invade Germany, and in doing so gave the King of Prussia an opportunity of invading France and of becoming Emperor of Germany. So much European history relates. But European history omits to mention that in that year Jack Miller fell in love, as far as it is possible at least for a youth of seventeen to fall. This was as important a page of history to him as the invasion of France to William von Hohenzollern. It was less important to the object of his admiration, though she too found amusement in it.

She was a barmaid at the Winterdale railway buffet. She was really pretty, and only three-and-twenty. Nothing particular came of it, except an inordinate expenditure on Jack's part on unwholesome food and beverages between meals, which the stomach of a 'man reading at Exeter's,' aged seventeen, could easily tolerate ; so the consequences were not as serious as mothers might fear and doctors hope.

The idea of marriage flitted, perhaps, vaguely through his brain. It was, however, only what a *savant* calls 'a certain marshalling and re-marshalling of the atoms' in his cranial cavity, and never gave itself vent in articulate speech. In his literary lessons in the *gai science*, moreover, all the gay Lothario characters and French musketeers, and countless suchlike, held marriage in ridicule and aversion, and he felt that he must adhere to the lofty ideal thus portrayed, and not lower himself by travelling in the well-worn ruts of the wain of virtue and respectability. Such a step as marriage here, he had also, apart from the Don Juan affectation, sense enough to perceive to be not only impossible and to the public eye wrong, but what is more intolerable than wrong, ridiculous.

He occasionally presented a sketch to his barmaid, who admired them, and rather admired him, in a shallow way. She never went for walks with him, or committed herself in any way; and the Winterdale people knew little about Jack's affairs and cared less, though of this he was not aware. He fancied himself the observed of all observers.

After a few months she was called to some other bar, and Jack saw her face no more. Jack's heart was not broken, and the muddy depths of the neighbouring ponds were cleft by no suicidal plunge. Up to his eighteenth year, he had no more serious sentimental affair than this; and it was now decided that he had sufficiently advanced in learning to matriculate

at St. Audit College, in the university
usually described by Thackeray as 'Oxbridge,' though its manners and customs,
spirit and style of learning, have somewhat
developed and differentiated since the
days of Pendennis, Foker, Magnus Char-
ters, *et hoc genus omne.*

CHAPTER V.

JACK'S ACADEMIC LIFE.

> ' Vivat Academia !
> Vivant Professores !'
> *Old Students' Song.*

JACK had not the advantage of an uncle
like Major Pendennis to guard his moral
well-being, and introduce him to the
university. Even his father was too unwell
at the time of his starting to accompany
him, so he had to march into the world by
himself, armed with a letter of introduction to Dr. Scalpel, the then Professor
of Pathology at Oxbridge (Oxbridge,
unlike the sister university of Camford,
possessed an active Faculty of Medicine

and a large hospital), who promptly
asked him to dinner on his arrival, and
made him welcome to the new life, and
made him feel that he had a friend he
could respect and trust. Jack never forgot
the kindness of Professor Scalpel to a
freshman in a strange world.

As has been already hinted, Oxbridge
was not then what it was in the reign of
Thackeray and his friend George the
Fourth. The work was harder, more
extensive, and more rationally conducted
than in the old days, the average of culture
slightly higher, the general spirit rather
more secular. The advance of learning,
civilisation, and toleration had made the
tone of the insular university more
European, and some at least of the old
prejudices had fled into the eternal limbo
prepared for such things. One great
change had taken place almost before
Jack's very eyes, and one of which the

result was, that many now held lecture-
ships, fellowships, and professorships who
formerly would have been expelled, or
never allowed to enter, for their opinions.

Jack took with mighty zeal at first to
the dissecting-room and the laboratory.
His perceptions were keen, and his mind
intensely realistic, and these studies took
his fancy thoroughly.

It is not our intention to minutely
investigate and describe Jack Miller's
academic career. The moral to the story
would be difficult to find. A general
sketch will suffice to indicate the directions of his spiritual development in these
three or four years. In his first year, he
was an 'advanced thinker,' admired
Buddha and Confucius, and read trans-
lations of the Rig-Veda, and announced
that the '*Zeitgeist* had made him an
enfant du siècle.' This may have been
true. At any rate, it was an advantage to

be able to state the interesting fact in so many modern languages. After his first year, he saw through his own ambition little pieces of affectation, and began to look the great realities of nature and joy and woe in the face. He could find delight in the scarlet autumn blaze of a Virginian vine, or the dark, graceful, stiff-twigged fir-trees outlined against the green pallor of the western sky at his home, as well as in the refined and wearied sensuousness of the marble-faced Dionysos, with vine-leaves wreathing his drooped head in the Art Museum at Oxbridge, or in the less refined though perhaps equally weary legs of burlesque, 'moving to the music of passion, with a lithe and lascivious regret,' in a Hall of Varieties in Leicester Square. For, be it remembered, a university education is incomplete in these latter days without frequent visits to the Metropolis, and to the various 'shrines where a sin is a prayer.' He was completely of the earth, earthy, and was not ashamed of it, but considered it as a natural and inevitable fact that he should be so. He said: 'If I ought to be otherwise than I am, I should have been made otherwise. I am a man, and act as fully as possible up to my nature. What else can you expect ?'

He attended his college chapel occasionally. This fact, combined with his home religious education, possibly in some part accounts for the dislike he felt to the popular religion of England. For irreligious, it is to be feared, Jack Miller certainly was, and, lamentable as it may sound, found many congenial spirits at Oxbridge who sincerely and entirely disbelieved everything that deans hold sacred.

He got to have friends of all sorts and descriptions, Christian and Parsee, German

and French, industrious and idle, worthless
and worthy ; but gradually, in the lapse of
time, he got more intimate with what some
called the 'modern fast set.' This was
a small circle, and utterly distinct from
the ancient fast set, which is composed of
rich or noble idlers, appetitous athletes *et
hoc genus omne,* and which is as old and
respected an academic institution as the
'varsity sermon.

No. Jack's friends were men of
moderate, some less than moderate,
means, who worked hard, mostly in his
own line of study, some senior and some
junior to himself, possessing plenty of
talent and wit, little or no religion, and
delighting in the ancient classics, Shakespeare, the Elizabethan and Restoration
dramatists, Théophile Gautier, Baudelaire
Hugo, and a certain school of modern
English poets : not that they were all
alike, of course, in these respects—a general

and suggestive type merely is here portrayed.

The man with whom Jack was perhaps
most of all confidential and intimate was
one Maximilian Laurence, the son of an
English doctor who wedded a Hungarian
actress at Vienna. He had studied at the
university of Vienna, as representing a
cheap and enjoyable life, for a few years,
and then, on the strength of his excellent
English and his good education, came to
seek, and won, a scholarship at St. Audit's,
Oxbridge, at his father's advice. His
father gave him an infinitesimal allowance,
and left him to cast his own nets in the
world's fishery. At Audit, of course,
living was a different matter to what it
was in Austria. But here the organism
managed to adapt itself to the environ-
ment, and got literary employment in
London, which, together with the scholarship, gave him a tolerable subsistence.

He was some years older than Jack, and possessed more experience of the world, and had more pronounced opinions in consequence. He was naturally endowed with a capacity for languages, and was familiar with all Jack's favourite authors, and a great many more beside. He appreciated nature, music, and poetry keenly, and they seemed to be the romantic element in his nature, and the symptoms of the Hungarian blood. Perhaps it was his Teutonic education that was responsible for his attachment to pure reason and free speculation, unfettered by the authority of men's opinions and traditions. The English element in his composition came out in his love of comfort, of cavendish, and of Shakespeare.

In the details of the political and religious disputes of the day he took but slight interest. He was not overjoyed or afflicted at the existence of an Established Church in

England, though he thought it contrary to the principles of pure reason. He said :

'If I hoped or struggled to see England governed by pure reason, I should wear out my body and mind, and leave England such as I found it.'

If you replied to him that if everyone used such arguments there would be no progress at all, he would say :

'Perhaps. But everyone does not use such arguments.'

As long as there existed good theatres, painters, musicians and poets, tobacco, girls and beer, he said an Established Church or an established anything else in no way affected the stream of his life. And a sparkling, joyous, and intelligent stream it was. He enjoyed life intensely, and almost every man and woman who knew him liked him, and every animal.

He was quite fearless in enunciating his opinions, though he did not do so on un-

called for occasions, and was careful to
avoid giving unnecessary offence in his talk.
To sum Maxmilian Laurence up, he was
one of those keen-minded, strong-bodied,
refined and enlightened young beings of this
latter day, for whose existence we may
largely thank, if thanks be due, the authors
of the new revolution—Voltaire, Goethe,
Musset, Heine, and multitudinous others,
whose names will readily occur to the
reader, whose chief ally, it may be added,
in the spiritual regeneration (or revolution,
whichever the reader likes) may be safely
asserted to be the older mediæval spirit
that so often asserts itself in fierce abuse
against them.

Some of Laurence's Oxbridge friends
called him 'Der Geist der stets verneint;'
and others, 'Der Kritik der reinen Ver-
nunft.'

His influence enlarged Jack's literary
taste, and stimulated him to study the

works of those whom Heine calls the
'children of light,' and 'soldiers in the
liberation war of humanity.'

He also introduced Jack to the circle of
rather Bohemian friends he possessed in
London, and showed him a few of the realities of that jovial, happy-go-lucky or
unlucky life, of which he had hitherto
gleaned his ideas from books.   Jack began
to have a real affection for the tall and
dingy streets of Bloomsbury, the Totten-
ham Court Road, and the strange half-foreign
cafés and restaurants, of which there are so
many, where good cookery and economy
prevail, and remembered many years after
the reckless, shag-smoking, lager-drinking,
song-making men—authors, actors, medical
students, aye, and actresses as well—that
he had known in his student days. Through
Max Laurence, Jack came to see a good
deal of a rather strange and not un-attrac-
tive section of human society, though it is

doubtful if his parents would have felt all the gratitude to his guide that Jack himself felt. So progressed his academic life. It is unnecessary to do more than just give one real extract from his career there, tending to give more definite ideas of Oxbridge and its associations for Jack than would be given by pages of description. To this a separate chapter is due, which will bring us to the termination of his third academic year, and the twenty-first and twenty-second of his life.

CHAPTER VI.

ALMA PIA—DURA MATER.

'It is just possible to become tired of Oxbridge, isn't it?' asked Jack of Max, as they walked slowly arm-in-arm, in the dusk of a March evening, towards the latter's rooms, where he had invited a few friends to a sort of formal farewell assemblage, previous to their both leaving Oxbridge, and subsequently to their both having taken their degrees.

'I think it is possible at certain moments to absolutely hate it,' the other replied. 'However, this is our last *Bummel* in these streets. Let us look at it with a kindly and pitying eye.'

It was a Saturday evening, about half-past eight, and the sky was clear and star-lit after a very wet afternoon, which had left a thin layer of sticky, dark slime on the pavement, interrupted at intervals by a puddle glittering in the gaslight, through which the numerous passers-by splashed carelessly. The large gutters, for which Oxbridge is so famous, were filled to over-flowing with rushing clear water, and the oath of some one accidentally treading in one was occasionally audible.

Jack and Laurence were in a long irregular street which extends from the heart of the town to its uttermost outskirt, and whose pavement in the evening, par-ticularly Saturday evening, is usually crowded. At every step they were jostled by old peasants in long smock-frocks, who were going home from their marketing, usually slightly unsteady from beer and gin ; undergrown youths from shops, from workrooms, and heaven knows where else; young women from the low suburb of Watergate, whose anæmic and hectic complexions, and attempts at fashionable attire, and audacious expressions, contrasted strongly with the coarsely healthy, thickly-built, red-faced countrywomen, also returning from market, some on foot, some in jerky carts with bad springs and much-whipped horses; and groups of university students, mostly freshmen, walking slowly and looking round from time to time, occupying a great deal of pavement, wearing very soft, drooping caps, and occasionally turning into a public-house or billiard-room.

To the right or left, every now and then, between the late open shops, one could catch glimpses of narrow, tall, dusky passages, with dark indications of clothes hung out to dry across them; generally also containing a group of two or three young girls, leaning with their backs to the wall, talking, laughing, and addressing remarks of a personal and ' chaffy ' nature to passing students. Now and then a hussar was visible, from the neighbouring garrison-town of Shoredale, in a great cloak, with crimson legs showing under it much spur and swagger, and, of course, like the rest of the world on such an even ing, slightly drunk.

At one side of the street was the bril- liant gas-lit descent to a skating-rink, where the sounds of a bad piano and fiddle were faintly audible, playing a well-known and popular polka, nearly drowned in the grinding of the wheels of the skaters. If one were to glance inside, one would see a crowd of men in four-cornered caps, and girls set free from their shop-counters, etc., for the evening, going round and round their prescribed course, like the heavenly bodies, in a hot, gassy atmosphere, which appeared to have permanently deprived the poor, pale, deformed pianist of a complexion. In its entrance-passage more youths in square caps were to be seen, smoking cigarettes and drinking beer sent in large shining pewter pots from a neighbouring public-house. (As a matter of fact, there was always a 'neighbouring' public-house and a 'neighbouring' tobacconist in any part of Oxbridge.)

'By Jove!' said Jack, 'I think we really have slummed along these streets about enough. About as much as the exigencies of our education demand. It is rather terrible, isn't it, to think how much time men waste here?'

'Pity that idea doesn't occur to the would-be dissipated freshman a little earlier in his academic career,' said the other. 'Let's go home.'

And they went to Laurence's rooms in St. Audit's College—large, comfortable

rooms, with an artistic and refined look
about them, and containing a great number
of books and a piano. Laurence was an
enthusiastic and talented musician. Regiments of claret bottles were on a side-table,
flanked by squadrons of soda-water bottles.
On a table in the middle of the room were
large beakers of glass, borrowed from one
of the laboratories, to hold claret-cup,
which Laurence and Jack, denuded of their
coats, were hastening to make. The kettle
was boiling on the fire, and an empty china
bowl for the later manufacture of whisky-
punch was in the background. The
'groceries' strewed the table. The latter-
day paganism, with all its culture, does
not despise the ancient and jovial institutions of cup and punch and ringing song,
nor even pipes and tobacco, a box of which
was open on the table. Just as Laurence
had lit a magnificent German porcelain
pipe, with a stem of immense length, the

guests turned up in a noisy crowd, with pipes hanging from the corners of their mouths. A loud and confused conversation arose, medicine and examinations at first being the prevailing topic, until some one cried out :

'Oh, hang shop! We get enough in the day-time. There is a time for all things. *Tempus est dapibus.*'

'Yes,' said Jack. 'Decidedly damn skin-diseases and exams. There are a variety of other instructive topics. Fine arts, drama, girls, politics.'

'Politics are distinctly objectionable. Leave them to the Union,' said another voice.

Soon, the voice of a fiery little lecturer on anatomy, or prosector, was heard in a corner laying down the law, with an amusing ferocity, on the follies of theology, and sundry jocular remarks about deans and doctrines might be heard. A tall, bearded handsome man, who had just been giving his ideas on egoistic Hedonism, Hegal and 'uvver fings,' suddenly said :

'By the way, apropos of Hedonism, was anyone at Thompson's drunk, day before yesterday ?'

'No; were you ?'

'Oh yes. I am thinking of writing a "College Drinking-party" in emulation of George Eliot's "College Breakfast-party," which, as you all know, gives such a truly accurate and realistic notion of the way men converse, here, on such occasions.'

'What was the drunk like, Villars?' asked Jack; 'was it interesting, or was there anything original about it ? Rather surprised, you know, to hear that you should have connection with such a performance.'

'Well,' said Villars, 'it is not a frequent amusement of mine, as you are aware. Thompson, you know, has recently made a

valiant and praiseworthy attempt to take a
degree in honours, which has met with that
cruel form of repulse from the examiners,
popularly called a " plough." In honour
apparently of this, he decided to have a
" wine," and invited me among others. I
had no decent excuse for refusing, and
not to hurt his feelings, went. It was
crowded, as anything of that sort given in
lodgings is likely to be. There was a
great deal of the brutal athlete element
present, more particularly in the form of
Sloane. Know Sloane, don't you ? enor-
mous man whose rooms are furnished
principally with rowing and athletic
photos ?'

'I know,' said Jack ; 'great pal of Lily
Jones of the Pig and Whistle bar, in
Watergate Lane.'

'I know nothing of his amorous ex-
ploits, but I can readily suppose it. I
only know that he got fearfully on at this

entertainment I am speaking of very early in the evening, and it took many men and much labour to keep him within some bounds.'

'I believe that man will have D.T. soon,' said Jack ; 'he can't do an hour's reading without bottled beer, even in the morning. His fingers speak alcoholism in every attempt to lift a glass or light a pipe.'

'He amused himself for a few minutes,' continued Villars, 'in throwing chairs downstairs, and his conversation was of the most hair-raising description.'

'I'll bet it was,' said the little demonstrator of anatomy, taking his short black pipe from his mouth, and blowing an additional puff of the perfume of burnt shag through the already clouded atmosphere.'

'After a while, when one or two rather quiet men had gone, Dawkins went to the piano, and there were a series of songs, each more illustrative than the last of the unutterable, and the putrefaction of poetic idea with which the undergraduate mind, in vinous moments, is capable of solacing itself.'

' I wish some one would cause a wave of oblivion to obliterate utterly, those " rhymes " and *Sporting Gazette* anecdotes from the brain of man,' observed Laurence. ' Anything more depressing could scarcely be conceived than the effect of hearing them over and over again from the mouths of different men, all alike in their brainless, shapeless want of originality.'

' I think some men's brain-cavities are filled with marmalade, or putty, or some equally potent composition,' observed the demonstrator.

' Sloane runs to cerebellum a good deal,' said Jack.

' The most exciting part of the per-

formance was getting Sloane home,' went
on Villars. 'He had firmly decided, with
that determination which is so strong in a
drunken man, that going home was a
foolish and unnecessary proceeding, and
argument and persuasion had very little
effect. He placed his great back against a
wall, and set his beastly dog at us. He
lives in some back street, to which the
route is rather involved, and it took some
three quarters of an hour before we could
get him into the hands of a philanthropic
policeman somewhere in his neighbourhood, who promised to see him home. I
hope he enjoyed the job.'

'I hope it hasn't demoralised you, and
given you that taste for vinous excess
Horace so viciously encourages?' asked
Jack.

'I hope not. When are you going
down ?'

'To-morrow morning. This is—I say it

with some feeling, made up of a little pride, some pain, and much satisfaction— the last night of my Oxbridge career. Max and I go to town to-morrow.'

' 'The devil you do !' said Villars. 'Where you are going to be Faust and Mephistopheles, Max and Moritz, companions in iniquity, I suppose.'

' 'Oh yes, go on Villars : David and Jonathan, Crosse and Blackwell, Hell and Tommy,' cried some voice from the corner of a sofa.

' We have what the knights of old called a quest,' said Laurence, ' to follow for a few days. After that, *Cras ingens— scire nefas.*'

' What's the quest in this case ?' asked the demonstrator, with a smile in his dark, vivacious eyes.

> ' " Nous songeons qu'à nous réjouir ;
> La grande affaire est le plaisir." '

' And the nature of that pleasure ?'

VOL. I.   9

> ' "Soyons toujours amoureux
> C'est le moyen d'être heureux." '

'Ah, I went in for that sort of thing when I was your age.'

'Really? That must be about two years ago, when you were my present age.'

'You are very full of quotation to-night; what have you been reading?'

'A work entitled " M. de Pourceaugnac " by Molière. Would you like one more short moral lesson from the same?'

'I'm not very keen on it, but I suppose you will not be satisfied till you have emitted it.'

> ' "Aimons jusque au trépas
> La raison nous y convie
> Hélas ! si l'on n'aimait pas
> Que serait-ce de la vie !
> Ah ! perdons plutôt le jour,
> Qui se perdre notre amour." '

'Hear, hear !' said Jack.

'Almost thou persuadest me to be a heathen,' said Villars, 'on your pattern.'

'Thought you were one,' said Jack.

'I am afraid I'm not quite so advanced as you and " Der Geist der stets verneint."'

'Der Geist der stets verneint' hung up his pipe, and said :

'Will any oblige with music or song ?'

'Won't you yourself, Max ?'

'Well, I don't mind doing one thing to start you with, but I protest against occupying my own piano for long. I'll sing you a song—you must not mind if it is German. It is the song of a student taking leave of his comrades—leaving his student life, the fights, and songs, and beer, and Liebchen, to go homewards, and become a sober Philistine and professional man.'

And he sang 'Bemooster Bursche ziehe ich aus.' Others followed, and English ballads came, in whose chorus everyone could join, and the melody floated out by the open windows, and wandered through the still night, startling stray passers and policemen, for the rooms looked on to the street.

Between the songs came general refreshment and confused jocular conversation, in the midst of which Laurence began to make the punch, and a sprightly young Frenchman, after distinguishing himself in a contest with Jack with a pair of foils, sat down to the piano and began the well-known old song :

> ' " Mon père est à Paris,
>   Ma mère est à Versaille,
>   Et moi je suis ici
>   Me couchant sur la paille." '

Just as the deafening chorus of ' L'amour, la nuit comme le jour ' was being rendered by the whole force of the company, the punch was placed on the table, and the college porter came to the door to request mitigation of the row.

' Who sent you ?' asked Laurence.

' The master, sir !'

' Take this glass of punch for yourself, and tell the master, if he has any complaint to make to me he can make it in person at King's Cross to-morrow, at 11.30, where I shall be.   In any case, tell him to——'

' " ——faire
L'amour,
La nuit comme le jour !" '

shouted the multitude. The porter grinned, swallowed his punch and withdrew. Some one volunteered to drop a mouse through the letter-slit in the master's door, and was restrained with some difficulty from carrying out the project, which would have perilled his prospects rather, as he would be certain to be detected in his present condition.

Laurence filled glasses round, and the old English song ' Three Jolly Post-boys ' followed, and several more. Finally, ' Auld Langsyne ' was sung with very unsteady ‘Highland honours,’ and the party broke up, and went whooping home on a continuous slide, the street having frozen in the night. Max and Jack instantly calmed down, closed the piano, and sat pensively smoking in armchairs before the fire.

‘Strange ! isn’t it ?’ observed the former; ‘any visitor would have fancied himself strayed into a barrack or a private asylum, who had come here half an hour ago, and would never have guessed that some of the best and cleverest fellows in the ’varsity were here, joking, drinking punch, and generally raising Hades in the way they did. Villars will get a professorship of metaphysics in Scotland; Smith is a lecturer, and prosector and fellow of his college already ; the other men are going to get high places, if they have not got them, except you and I, who remain and lament Mimi Pinson, and the *temps perdu*.’

'It isn't *perdu* a bit,' said Jack. 'We've put twice the enjoyment and profit into our time that the senior wranglers and double-firsts, who go the same ground every afternoon and eat quarts of marmalade, have.'

'Perhaps. It's all over now, anyhow. We've done our little strut in bachelors' gowns, and have seen the best and the worst of Oxbridge; the best is not very good, and the worst is very brutal. I shall not forget the sights we have sometimes seen here, of unbridled authority exerting itself; of virulent virtue with bands and bull-dogs crushing venomous vice with such exemplary austerity that makes the hands tingle and the blood boil; we shall not forget the morality of our authorities, that permits the same man to fine you for smoking in the street, and to preside in the college hall at a boat-club drunk. We shall not forget the tutors whom we pay to do nothing except send us down if necessary, and the chaplains that make services a caricature of religion, and the deans who would force us to attend them.'

'And we shall not forget the few good friends we have made, and the real good times we have had.'

'Have you packed up?'

'No.'

'When do you mean to? Because the train's at ten, and you won't be in a hurry to rise to-morrow, "when later larks give warning;" the later lark being regarded as just over.'

'Oh, I'll manage in time. I'm not drunk, and there's a whole night yet.'

'Stay with me, and help make some anchovy toast and coffee.'

'It's one a.m. I'm not such a bird of night as you.'

'You'd better stay. I want to show

you some new books—Spinoza in Dutch
—linguistic exercise.'

'Spinoza be d——d, at this hour in the
morning; as he probably is from a theo-
logical standpoint. No, sir! I'm going
to pack and sleep—perchance to dream.
Then there's my tub! We will meet at
Philippi—that is to say, in my rooms, where
you will breakfast later in the course of
the morning. Good-night.'

'Good-night.'

And Laurence sat up reading Spinoza
among the remains of claret-cup, punch,
bits of lemon, and tobacco ashes.

CHAPTER VII.

ROSA ENTERS SOCIETY.

AFTER the German war, Dr. Taylor, on receipt of a letter from Césarine, and a posthumous one from Félix, written in case of his death, sailed for Europe *viâ* Hamburg, and went, as he said, 'as straight as railroad cars could take him' to the Rue de la Harpe, and the Boulevard St. Michel, and found Rosa, overjoyed to see him, grown into a tall, lithe girl of fourteen, with the experiences of war and starvation on her pale face and thin limbs, and looking at him with unlimited affection out of hollow large brown eyes. He at once prescribed tonics, food, and amusements, which soon restored her frame to its healthy *status quo ante bellum.*

Césarine had grown into a handsome, slightly faded woman between thirty and forty. Fourteen years had made little difference to Taylor himself. The man who looks forty at four-and-twenty does not usually look any older at eight-and-thirty.

As soon as Paris was habitable for ladies, Dr. Taylor's sister and brother-in-law, Colonel and Mrs. Maston G. Frankland, sailed also for Europe, *vià* Liverpool, and came to Paris, where the Colonel was attached to the American Legation.

Dr. Taylor, observing that Rosa was rapidly turning from a girl of fourteen into a woman of fifteen, determined, to his own infinite regret, and to that of Césarine, and of Rosa herself, that it was time for her to leave the Quartier; and he looked after some protector of her own sex, more efficient, though none could be more willing or kind-hearted, than Césarine. He explained this to the latter as delicately as possible, and she assented, with some tears, on the condition that she was to be occasionally visited by Rosa.

So Rosa was transferred to the care of Mrs. Maston Frankland, who was the acme of elegance and propriety, and who, after listening to the true story of Rosa, as told by her brother—who, in his direct, simple-minded way, expected the same enthusiastic approval from this lady-like sister of his that he got from Césarine, the brasserie waitress—said :

' Well, if you ain't the oddest kind, Ivor ! However, I suppose I must try what I can do.'

Mrs. Frankland was too weak to refuse to do what she was even slightly unwilling to do. Taylor went on, in a hesitating voice :

'Say, you'll dress her properly, won't you—way other smart girls are dressed? I'll stand that; and, see here, she's learnt a whole crowd of things already—I don't know that it's exactly necessary that she should go to school—see?'

'I see.'

'And you'll give her a good time, as much as you can?'

'I'll try.'

And Rosa came, shy and anxious-looking, to a new and, to her eyes, magnificent quarter of Paris, and drove about in one of those carriages she had sometimes admired and envied, as they splashed her while crossing the Boulevard des Capucines. Mrs. Frankland liked Rose in her own gelatinous, lazy way, but was a little afraid of her direct fearless eyes, and direct fearless questions and sayings. Rosa had been brought up to habits of outspoken sincerity from the example of Taylor himself, and it made Mrs. Frankland lament that she had not had the charge of her sooner, so as to have made her more 'elegant' and 'high-toned' in her opinions. She resolved that it must be still possible to reform Rosa, and turn her into an elegant and high-toned girl, with proper respect for rank and fashion and money. She believed in dollars, did Mrs. Frankland, and had plenty of them, and had no objection to expending them on Rosa's improvement. She firmly believed that money, generously and judiciously laid out, could, in some mysterious way, instil a spirit of proper opinion and proper reverence for great and good things, such as dresses, dinners, dances and dollars, into Rosa's mind, and resolved to have a consultation with her friend the Marquise de Tortoleone on the subject.

The Marquise de Tortoleone, on her marriage, was not the prettiest woman in

Paris ; but she thought she was, and years failed to dispel the illusion. She was four-and-twenty at the time of her discovery by the Marquis, which is really rather young for a married woman, and passes readily for nineteen for some years with judicious management. Her personal appearance was undoubtedly striking, as the Marquis was aware to his cost—to his cost advisedly ; for a striking face and figure require, as no one can dispute, striking dresses and decorations as auxiliaries, which must be frequently varied, and always half an inch ahead of the prevailing fashion. They attract, moreover, the notice of the world, and a moth-like crowd of male worshippers and *cavalieri servente* calculated to disturb the peace of mind of a husband.

Fortunately for the Marquis, it took a good deal to disturb his mental equanimity. He was distinctly aware that all pecuniary

supplies were under his control, and that
the Marquise's love of flirtation was too
universal, and her discretion too great, to
permit her, under the circumstances, to go
in any sense too far. Besides, he could
find means of consoling himself, while
living so long apart from her and un-
noticed by her, as he generally did.

The Marquis was French. Before he
became, by right of purchase, the possessor
of the Italian estate and title of Tortoleone,
his name had been Jean Bouvier. He was
a lucky speculator, a man ignorant in all
matters outside the Bourse, and in society
the perfection of snobbery. The Bourse
was his Paradise, and the demoniac yells of
the frequenters of that institution were to
him as angels' songs. The god he wor-
shipped was called 'Rentes,' and was a
near relation, with modern improvements,
of the deity to which Shadrach, Meshach,
and Abednego refused to bow down on the

plain of Dura. Society sneered at him'
but tolerated him. His means were an
apology for his manners. He knew the
celebrity one can gain from being the pro-
prietor of a pretty wife, when one can
afford to pay M. Worth and his like to
dress her, and, on the strength of this
knowledge and his own affluence, he went
into the 'Babylonian market,' and, after
some bargaining, procured the article required. The new speculation was a
success. People grew tired of asking who
the Marquise was, because no one could
answer the question. But she was undeniably a beauty. After looking at her and
talking to her in a surprised and almost
reverent way for a few days, the Marquis
returned to his old love, the Bourse, and
left his wife to amuse herself in her own
way, which she was not slow to do. In
due time the Marquise became the mother
of a son. This was Alfred de Tortoleone,

who has been noticed slightly in a former chapter.

After five years of conjugal bliss, the Marquis disappeared entirely, leaving a polite note to say that pressing business required his immediate presence in a part of the world which he vaguely described as 'the East.' The uncharitable, and particularly his creditors, hinted that the business alluded to was carried on in the Levant, or consisted in raising a harem somewhere in Roumelia. The affliction of the Marquise at his loss was not overwhelming, and was alleviated by the fact that he had settled a comfortable income on her, on her wedding-day. She showed a glimmer of common sense by sending her boy to be educated in England, saying that if he were sent to a French school he would grow up an insufferable little fool: a rash prediction, perhaps, and founded on a hasty generalisation from the particular Parisian young gentlemen under the Empire with whom she happened to be acquainted. Therefore Alfred, in due time, became an English schoolboy, and an object of curiosity and diversion to his companions. Not because there was anything particularly curious or diverting about him, but because he was a foreigner. He arrived, by the way, with the impression that he would be addressed as 'Marquis,' and was somewhat surprised to find that a vile and vulgar foreign democracy at once named him 'Frenchy,' varied occasionally by the equally witty and pungent nickname of 'Froggy.' He very soon became as English and commonplace as any of them. Jack Miller, who was his schoolfellow, was supposed to look after and protect his young cousin, which we will hope he did.

The Marquise was addicted to reading

witty comedies and 'proverbes,' and fancied herself to resemble the charming and epigrammatic marquises and countesses with which they were populated. She had a 'salon' and receptions, and endeavoured to be a species of female Mæcenas. She was not unpopular. Her talents were few, but the greatest of them was one of a nature calculated to win popularity.

This was a marvellous capacity of simulating an enthusiasm for whatever might interest the person she was conversing with, and dexterously inserting compliments at the same time. Her friends called this capacity amicability and large-mindedness. It was what is known in the Sister Isle as 'blarney,' and in this country by the more downright if more coarse name of 'humbug.'

It was to this lady that Mrs. Frankland went for advice in her difficulty about Rosa, and laid her case confidently before her. The Marquise said she perfectly comprehended the whole situation, and advised the sending of Rosa to a conventual educational institution with which she was acquainted. This was just what Mrs. Frankland wanted an excuse and encouragement for doing, and the Marquise soon persuaded her that it would be a most benevolent act, and one in no way coming under Dr. Taylor's prohibition anent schools. The two ladies embraced, and parted with expressions of mutual esteem. Rosa was unsuspectingly led to suppose, in a vague way, that she was going where Dr. Taylor thought proper, and entered this pension, conducted by *réligieuses.*

The brilliant success of this step on Mrs. Frankland's part may be surmised from the following letter from the Mother Superior, received a week after the entrance of Rosa, which reached Mrs.

Frankland at breakfast, sent her into wild dismay and disarray :

'CHÈRE MADAME,

'Mademoiselle your ward has this afternoon left us, after defiantly refusing to perform a punishment set her, on the plea that it was unjust; which assertion in the mouth of one of her years to her superiors, is in itself an act of insubordination. Where she has gone I know not; but, dear Madame, I feel it my painful duty to add, that finding Mademoiselle Rosa Taylor to be without religion, or a distinct code of disciplinary morality, I cannot readmit her here, as such a step would imply the total demoralisation of my other charges, who have already a tendency to sympathise with the rebellious conduct of Mademoiselle Taylor.

'Agree, Madame, my considerations the most distinguished, and believe me,

'Your always devoted

'OLIVIA, *Mère Supérieure.*'

This missive Mrs. Frankland looked at as if it were an obus that had sailed in at the window, and exploded on the break-fast-table. It was quickly followed by an irruption of heavy infantry, in the form of Dr. Ivor Taylor, who stood with his back to the fire, and said in a gentle, low drawl:

'Now see here, Alexandra G. Frankland. I believe I told you it would not be neces-sary to send Rosa to a boarding-school. I imagine you assented to that proposition. Is that so?'

'I didn't send her to a boarding-school.'

'If you will draw the delicate distinction that divides a boarding-school from a con-ventual pension you will be more clever than I ever took you for. I guess it's some smarter person than you that thought of that scare.'

'It *is* different, anyway.'

'It *is*, a little. But the difference is for the worse. If Rosa ain't educated enough,

I don't mean to have the finishing of her run by nuns—see? I have given her over to you to have her kept pure, and if that is your notion of how to do it, she might just as well come back to the Quartier. I don't suppose it's your fault. Your mind ain't strong enough to take such a decided step alone, but I'm particularly grateful to whoever put it into your head, and would like to have an opportunity of expressing my feelings to her — it must be her — a man wouldn't be such a—— Well, all right. I'm not going to cuss, don't put on that scared face. Do you like Rosa? Do you and she get along together?'

'I like her very much. I think she likes me.'

Mrs. Frankland here sobbed.

Her brother said :

'I've seen a good many cases of hysteria and weeping women, in hospitals and out of 'em, and they don't alter my feelings

much by now. If you want to have Rosa
back, you shall; but on the distinct under-
standing that you keep her with yourself.
She did quite right to leave that place you
sent her to, and an elegant scare she's
given them. They don't quite know what
a Yankee-bred girl means yet, there, I
fancy—kind of new and dangerous animal;
might encourage the French girls to be
riotous and playful, and shy their rosaries
at one another's heads. Perhaps you'll
write to them to send back her traps. I've
already sent them the stamps for the
quarter's pay, so they can't complain that
Rosa defrauded them any. Do you understand me?'

'Yes.' (Mrs. Frankland was frightened,
thrown off her dignity, and thoroughly
subdued.) 'Well, I'll send her back.'

Rosa came back. The only remark she
ever condescended to make about her short
school experience was: 'They all liked

me ; the girls, I mean. I believe they thought I was a sort of boy.'

She and Mrs. Frankland got used to one another in time, and got on quietly and amicably. Rosa soon understood her guardian. Mrs. Frankland soon gave up trying to understand Rosa.

A few years later, when Rosa became sixteen, Colonel Frankland suddenly died; and Mrs. Frankland, at the recommendation of her mentor, the Marquise, determined to go to England.

CHAPTER. VIII.

DOMESTIC.

JACK AND HEL MILLER were sitting together in the room consecrated by the former to the pursuit of the fine arts and the consumption of tobacco. It was about a quarter to midnight on Easter-eve. Jack had come home after taking his degree, and enjoying a few days and nights of festivity with Laurence and other friends in London, and was for the present reposing on his laurels, or rather on a rocking-chair, and sucking pensively at a large dark-looking pipe. He had invited Hel to assist him in discussing his next step, or rather to form an audience while he pointed out to her the merits and demerits of various schools of medicine, and laid down the law on other things on which she was not competent to dispute.

He was determined to go to Paris ; and when he was determined that a thing should happen, it somehow generally did happen. Having announced his various projects and their reasons, and discovered the way in which his parents were likely respectively to regard them, he went on to more general matters, in which Hel could take a greater interest. Laurence was expected at Eave Lodge next day. Jack had to answer numerous questions about him, and give a minute description of him to his sister.

'I wonder if I shall like him ?' said she.

'I fancy you will: you ought. Most girls only care as long as a man is good-looking. Max is undeniably good-looking, and has got some wits as well.'

'What a strange way you have of talking of " most girls," as if they were a class of inferior animal whose habits you had been studying !'

'Just the state of the case. And very nice little animals they are ! What have they done to prove the contrary ? I grant you they have ambition—Lucifer's own ; but what does it produce ? Members of school-boards, Girtonites in sap-green with silver chains round their wrists and double eye-glasses. I believe in the higher culture of women, because it makes them more agreeable to men. They recognise themselves, perhaps unconsciously, the truth in a certain sense of the saying, " The woman was made for the man." One of the most prominent female artists of our country devotes herself to the glorification on canvas of men, particularly men engaged in an unintellectual and savage profession.'

'But soldiers needn't be unintellectual !'

'Who mentioned soldiers ? However, as you have assumed, presumably from the accuracy of my description, that I meant soldiers, I may add that I didn't say soldiers were necessarily without intellect. I said that the profession was eminently savage, a profession only existing in virtue of the imperfection of civilisation, like that of the clergy——'

'Oh, Jack !'

'Like that of the clergy, and consequently only advancing men's minds in the direction of ingenuity of destruction or subjugation of other men, mind and body—the soldiers the body, the clergy the mind.'

'I don't think that's quite fair.'

'Well, no, perhaps not. I apologise to all your military and clerical partners in waltzes or lawn-tennis, for undue heat. Talking of undue heat reminds me that this is an uncommonly warm April, and that that is an uncommonly ditto fire, and I mean to open the window.'

Jack got up from his rocking - chair, heavy meerschaum pipe in mouth (a birthday present that five chorus-maidens of the Park Lane Theatre had once subscribed for), stretched, looked in the glass that hung over the mantelpiece, and walked over to the window, drew up the venetian blinds, opened both windows, leaned on the sill of one, and gazed out. The full moon was behind the grove of firs in the west, among streaks of horizontal cloud. The trees were black, distinct and beautiful, as he had seen them at times before. That sight was an embodiment to him of his whole childhood and youth, spent in reach of that grove. In the distance lay a black foggy mass with dots of light in it, having a squarish protuberance in its middle. This was Winterdale and its cathedral; fields and downs were moderately bright, going away into grey and foggy perspective. Above all was the starlit sky.

'Come and look at all this, Hel!' Jack was drinking in the wonderful though melancholy and thought-bringing beauty of the scene.

Hel came to the window-sill alongside him, and looked out.

'*Es stehen unbeweglich die Sterne in der Höhe,*' quoted Jack. 'Heine might have known,' he added, laughing; 'that the stars are not immovable at all. However, they are immovable to human joy and sorrow. In his sense it is true. They are the pitiless and passionless eyes of heaven.'

'That doesn't sound quite original, some-how,' observed Hel gently.

Jack looked at his watch.

'Three minutes past twelve. One

begins to feel like Faust. It is Easter morning. Let us listen for the chorus of angels.' And they were both momentarily silent. A long low wailing shriek came borne upon the still air, from some distance. Hel started, and said :

'What's that ?'

'The mail coming into Winterdale. Seven minutes late, too. I should think you might know a railway whistle this time in the nineteenth century. So much for that century's answer to Faust.'

'I think the nineteenth century has advanced to that stage properly called bed-time,' said Hel. 'Wait till my pipe's done. Well, yes, I'll go to Paris. Necessary part of my education—also to bed, necessary part of my physical maintenance—to sleep, perchance to dream —perchance not.'

These short, disjointed remarks were emitted alternately with smoke-clouds.

Jack then carefully knocked out and otherwise extracted ashes and oily refuse from his pipe, stroked it with a silk handkerchief, and laid it in its case.

'I think you'll like Max,' he said, as they separated for the night.

'Perhaps I shall. I hope so. Good-night.'

Just at this time another conclave had been dissolved in another smoking-room, or rather study in which smoking was practised. Professor Miller sat in his writing-chair, in a dressing-gown, with a long German pipe in his hand. Opposite to him on the wall, was a copy of Rembrandt's 'Anatomy Lesson.' Around the walls stood shelves bearing bottles of what Mrs. Miller and Hel called 'things,' in spirits, which gave the room a vague air of alchemy, the Black Art, and general horror to unscientific Winterdale. Of course there was a book-case, with several skulls—infant, pre-historic, negro, and the inevitable 'Ancient Briton'—on its top. One or two pairs of *schlägers*, another German pipe, and a photograph of Heidelberg Castle, were the only other adornments of the walls. The room was in a mysterious twilight, which a decaying fire and a setting moon united to produce, and was not wholly unlike the opening scene of Faust, except that it was not Gothic, and the occupant had a rather contented humorous expression, and was, with nineteenth-century irreverence, smoking Dutch Kanaster tobacco, instead of meditating on the eternal unfitness of things.

He was also aware that it was Eastereve, and past midnight, and was delivering a discourse on Faust to Mrs. Miller, who wanted to go to bed.

'There is an immense deal in what you say, Nellie. Going early to bed is an excellent rule, and one I never observe.

If Faustus had gone to bed at the proper time, instead of talking blank verse all night about things he didn't understand, matters would have taken a very different course, and a great deal of misfortune would have been averted. He would have discovered the elixir of life, and swallowed a dose. The funeral would probably have taken place next day, and the will would have been found to devise his whole hypothec, consisting of a furnace, two skulls, his manuscripts, and a small phial of poison, with directions 'for internal application,' to Wagner—who would richly deserve it all, particularly the last item. Gretchen would have continued to attend public worship, clothed in a white dress and a bag, and would have married some respectable young Philister, who also habitually went to church, and would have been the mother of twelve children. Valentine would have lived to be a general,

and would come home and tell stories of
the wars to his nephews and grand-
nephews—fine old crusted lies which they
knew by heart, and he nearly believed at
last himself. What ?'

'I thought you were going to talk about
Jack.'

Poor Mrs. Miller had patiently borne
the comparative merits of German and
English poetry, and incidentally pipes;
some funny remarks about the Bishop of
Winterdale, which somehow contrived to
get into the conversation, and the importance of visceral arches in relation to the
segmentation of the skull; and finally Faust,
as a last straw, hoping all the time that he
would give her an opportunity of uttering
advice and predictions concerning Jack.

'Jack? He wants to go to Paris. I
suppose he'd better go in the autumn.'

'Don't you think it rather a mistake to
let him go so far by himself, and so unpro-

tected, into the way of all sorts of temptations ?'

'He would have just as much temptation in London, and of a less civilised kind. He must learn medicine somewhere, and it can't very well be here.'

'Couldn't we go to Paris, too, for a while? It would do Hel good to get an outing, and we could then have Jack with us.'

'And keep an eye on him, and see that he doesn't go to theatres on Sundays? He'd thank you. You didn't want to keep an eye on him at Oxbridge?'

'But that is England, and so different.'

'Unless Oxbridge has altered, largely since my time, there are just as good opportunities there as anywhere for transgression of all laws moral and divine. Temptations, as people are pleased to call them, are to be met with in large numbers.

Yet Jack does not appear to be hopelessly depraved. He is rather conceited, though not conspicuously so, and has learned a good deal since he went there, and has altogether developed, mentally and physically, into a more presentable member of society.'

'Of course I have some confidence in him; and his principles I hope are still strong in him, though he is very irreligious.'

'Well, can't you extend that confidence across the Channel, and along the Chemin de Fer du Nord, as far as Paris?'

Mrs. Miller's fear for, and confidence and pride in, Jack were struggling together; and she finally gave in, as she invariably did, to her husband, and fetched a bedroom candle. As she was lighting it, the Professor said:

'I say, there's that young fellow that Jack expects to-morrow; we ought to do

something for his amusement.   Let's invite
the Franklands to dinner.'

'We'll see.'

And Eave Lodge slept.

CHAPTER IX.

MAX LAURENCE.

ON Easter-day, a brilliant day, with an east wind and dust, Mrs. Miller and Hel deserted Mr. Exeter's church in the morning for the cathedral at Winterdale. As they came out of it, at the end of the service, they met two young men, in ulsters and hard round felt hats, with pipes in their mouths.

One of these was Laurence, the other was Jack. The former asked the latter in an undertone, 'Who is that?' as he saw Hel, in a new olive-green costume, looking quietly charming, with that submissive sort of expression that young ladies wear on Sundays, and slightly flushed with the warm, impure atmosphere of the crowded cathedral, and just in that kitten-like pursuit of her train which always took place at church doors.

Jack replied by approaching his relations and saying :

'Allow me to introduce Mr. Laurence ; —my mother and sister.'

Max hastily pocketed a hot pipe and took off his hat. Mrs. Miller asked him if his luggage were disposed of, and Jack explained that it had gone on to Eave Lodge, and that they proposed walking home. Mrs. Miller engaged Laurence in a conversation about the weather and his journey, and Jack talked to Hel.

Max's last remark to Jack had been :

'You know, it is an entirely new experience to me to be in an English family residence. I don't know how I shall behave. You must tell me if I commit any solecisms.'

Jack had replied :

' Oh, I think you will find you have not fallen among the Philistines.'

Max Laurence was just a little puzzled and afraid at first of Mrs. Miller, but soon became comfortable on finding in her the quiet kindness and good-nature of a really good Englishwoman, described in the recognised slang of the age as a 'lady.' To her, Laurence was a rather striking, foreign-looking young man, who spoke directly to the point, and was not embarrassed, though a little shy. She soon got him to talk about Vienna by observing :

' I think you have lived a good deal abroad, have you not, Mr. Laurence ?'

' I am a Hungarian or an Englishman by birth,' replied he, ' whichever you like. My father was English and my mother

Magyar. I was a student for some two or three years in Vienna.'

Mrs. Miller then talked about Vienna, and society there, and scenery, in a general way. She had been there once for a week, and made excursions into the environs. Scenery Laurence knew a good deal about, and the features of the neighbourhood. Society he knew only by sight and reputation (or the absence of it), but as Mrs. Miller did not know even that much, he was equal to the situation. He said :

'You see, a student does not know any society in the English sense, unless he is a prince, or very noble, or very rich, and I was none of these. But I can be a guide-book to you to every café, theatre, promenade, and music and art curiosity in the place, if you should wish to obtain information before visiting Vienna again; but I dare say you know much of this already.'

'I am afraid not much. And how do you like Oxbridge? Jack seems very well pleased with it. I should think it must be rather different to you after Vienna.'

'I thought so, certainly. At first, the costumes and the ancient character of the place struck and enchanted me. I seemed to have lighted on an island of Middle Age in the midst of a sea of Nineteenth Century. I soon found that the form only was mediæval, and the spirit modern. Modern, at least, after allowing for insular peculiarities of idea and method of study and amusement. There seems still to be a great deal of religious spirit in existence, however, for a modern university.'

This was a slip of Max's, as he felt the moment he had said it. He thought: 'How could I say this to a woman just coming out of an English cathedral on a

Sunday !' and waited anxiously for the result.

'Well, I hope so,' said Mrs. Miller, 'though I am afraid there is none too much of it. I suppose there is very little religion in the German universities ?'

'Oh, very little, except in the faculties of theology, it always seemed to me,' replied this young philosopher, in a calm and satisfied tone. 'I think,' he added, 'they are at a stage of thought in England which has already been gone through by Germany.'

Here Mrs. Radford passed with a bow and a sweet smile, and explained to her husband, at lunch, that those Millers had got a queer-looking young man with them ; and that young Miller smoked pipes on Sunday, and close to the cathedral door too ; and that she was so sorry for them, as she had a real regard for Mrs. Miller. But it was to be expected, when their

parish clergyman was a Ritualist, and
Dr. Miller was an infidel, or the next
thing to it.

Mrs. Miller talked then of English
country life, of which Max knew nothing,
and was fully prepared to enjoy, mud and
all ; and so conversing, they arrived at
Eave Lodge, with which the young
stranger was charmed. The Professor
welcomed him cordially, and said lunch
was waiting. Mrs. Miller said it had been
so beautiful out of doors, that they had
not liked to hurry through it. Hel went
upstairs to take off her 'things.' Jack took
charge of his friend, and the Professor
stood on the grass outside, looking at the
sunshine, which glittered through his long
grey hair, and showed every detail of his
wrinkled but grand old face. He walked
up and down with hands in his pockets.
He was still lame, permanently so, it
seemed, but not severely. He was dressed

in an old brown suit, which might be called a shooting-suit, if there had been the slightest trace of evidence to show that he had ever shot anything in his life, except a fox that once managed to effect a raid on Hel's chickens when she was a small girl. (Which action, it is hardly necessary to remark, confirmed the county gentry in the opinion that 'that' Miller was a beastly Radical and an Atheist.)

He was wondering why the pelvic girdle in some fish is anterior to the pectoral, at this moment, and also why an east wind was so detrimental to the equanimity of his temper. These questions occupied him until the lunch-bell rang. Hel fetched him in.

During the meal they all had an opportunity of studying their guest. Mrs. Miller was relieved to find that he ate with a fork, and did not look surprised when it and his knife were renewed at each course, her notions of German habits and customs being derived from *tables-d'hôte*. She saw in Laurence a well-man-nered, well-informed young man, with a pleasant face, and perhaps slight symptoms of rather advanced ideas, with a quiet, self-convinced decision about most things that he said that sometimes surprised her.

Hel, of course, noticed his appear-ance first. This was not of a style to which she was accustomed, but im-pressed her favourably, notwithstanding. She saw a pale, well-shaped face with a straight nose (which she described as Grecian subsequently), dark eyes, deeply placed under black eyebrows, a low wide forehead, and quantities of curly wavy black hair, rather longer than the prevail-ing fashion in England permitted. The mouth was a little wide, with good regular white teeth, and surmounted by a small black moustache, scarcely deserving the

name. Then his body, though thin, was
well-shaped, and his hands were white,
and his fingers long. When he talked
she thought he must be very clever, and
seemed to know a good deal about places
and subjects of which she knew very little.
This impressed her with a sense of his
superiority. In short, Hel approved of
the man instinctively, though she knew
very little about him.

The Professor thought Laurence was a
youth with some brains. He drew from
him information concerning the present
state of learning in Oxbridge, the personal
appearance now of this and that professor
in Germany whom he had known years
ago, and incidentally got scraps of opinion
from him on many topics, which made the
Professor say to himself:

'You'll some day run that good-looking
head of yours against the rock of British
Philistinism, young man, that Matthew

Arnold talks about.' After looking at
him, and listening to him a little longer,
the Professor mentally added, 'But I
shouldn't wonder if you made rather a hole
in that rock before it crushed you.'

Laurence, of course, was forming opinions
of his entertainers. They ran rather like
this (at least, this is how they appeared in
a letter of his to a confidential friend) :

'Herr Papa.—Professor ; a Scotchman.
Almost a "child of light"—eccentric,
paternal, and a man I really like.

'Frau Mamma.—Pleasant, kind, reli
gious—not very Philister, as English
mothers probably go.

'Die Mamsell Sœur.—An English girl,
pure and innocent, and moderately well-
educated—*hold und schön und rein.* Ought
to have more Goethe and Heine and
Grecism instilled into her, to counterbalance
the mediævalism of maternal teaching.
Religious, certainly, but more plastic

12—2

mind and younger ideas than mother ;
naturally comes of association with the
nineteenth-century brother.'

After lunch, Jack proposed going out of
doors to smoke, and asked Hel to come.

'Take a plaid, dear,' said Mrs. Miller ;
' you know there is an east wind '

Hel obtained a plaid, and set out with
her brother and Laurence for the fir-grove.
This rendered their tread silent, with its
carpet of reddish-brown fir-needles mixed
with broken branches and fallen cones.
Where the tall, stiff stems of the trees
were not covered with rough scaly bark,
they were light-red in the sunlight, where
it arrived at them through the interstices
of the branch-roof. They arrived at the
grey wooden five-barred frontier-gate, and
stopped and leaned on it, sheltered from
the wind. The three found themselves
looking westward and north-westward over
a far extending valley, with fields near

and woods and downs in the distance, looking far-off and still, with the warm spring mist upon them. Church-bells and sheep-bells were mingling together in the distance, calling their several flocks, as Jack irreverently remarked.

'Let us stay here awhile,' said he, immediately after this, 'and talk of something sensible, and take in the scenery.'

'I am not surprised,' said Laurence, after a long look at the prospect, 'that England has produced nature-poets like Shelley and Keats. And this is all so English. Except these fir-trees. They carry one to Germany, in the mind, quicker than the magic cloak of Mephistopheles. Have you been in Germany, Miss Miller?'

'I have been up the Rhine once. It was beautiful.'

'Did you read the Rhine stories and the " Nibelungen Lied" then ? That was the time to do it.'

'I am afraid my German was not good enough; and we had so many things to think about that we hadn't time to think at all.'

'We thought of time-tables, tariffs, and *tables-d'hôte* I believe principally,' said Jack.

'You read German, however, now?' asked Laurence of Hel.

'Yes; but I haven't read much. I read with a governess at first, and she didn't select the nicest pieces, I fancy. I don't suppose the "Thirty Years' War" is exactly the most interesting thing to a girl that Schiller ever wrote, and I had to read it. It took so long—almost as long as the war, I think—that I haven't had time to do much else but recover from it since.'

'Goethe?'

'The "Erl-König," set to the piano. The rest was pronounced beyond my—that

is, the governess's—powers of appreciation,
and often of doubtful moral tendencies.'

'Hel's governess,' said Jack, 'divided
German authors into two great classes—
the proper and the improper. Under the
first head came the "Thirty Years' War,"
and the "Tragedy of Wallenstein;" under
the second, the rest of Teutonic literature.'

'Now that you are emancipated,' went
on Max to Hel; 'will you not begin upon
a new ground—on that of freedom of
choice, guided by taste ?'

'I should like to; but I haven't got
any taste. It is all unknown country to
me. Where ought I to begin ?'

'If I might presume to advise, I should
say begin with Goethe's short songs and
poems. To me they convey the whole
beauty and art of Goethe, in his interpreta-
tion of life and nature, in a particularly
attractive way. With that, "Dichtung
und Wahrheit" as his best prose. Later,

when you have lived a little longer, you
will read Heine. You will not so much
care for him yet. He is Goethe's successor in literature.'

'I dare say I will begin soon,' replied
Hel. 'I think papa has Goethe's and
Schiller's works.'

'Probably. You have perhaps many
things to do in the household which occupy
your time, however? In Germany young
ladies do not have too much time to give
to literature.'

'I have been decorating the church a
good deal lately. It has occupied me
nearly all the morning and all the afternoon for several days. You see, there
were so few people to do it. We would
have made you help if you had been
there.'

'Decorate the church? What for?'
asked this young heathen.

Hel's turn to instruct now came.

'This is Easter Day, you know,' she explained gently, as one breaking some rather startling tidings to an unprepared person.'

'And you decorate your church at Easter ? How is it done ? Might I see it ?'

'Yes ; you can come this afternoon, if you like, when the service is over. We collect flowers and evergreens, make wreaths, bouquets and crosses, and arrange them about the church. Jack is made to go up very high ladders, to put up what we can't reach. Have you never been to an English church at Easter, Mr. Laurence ?' asked she suddenly, with an inexplicable feeling of sympathy for what was to her a strange and foreign variety of indefinitely dreadful outer darkness.

' I do not remember any such occasion,' replied he.

' Don't they decorate your chapels at

Oxbridge ? I should think it would be a nice occupation for you.'

' I am afraid it is not seen in that light at Oxbridge. I believe it is not usual to decorate college chapels ; but I cannot say for certain what deans, in their poetic and vacation moments, may be capable of doing. I seldom enter them myself.'

' Will you come to church with us some day, here ?' asked Hel.

Max was in a dilemma. Pure reason within him said : ' Going to church is a performance which you must admit to be idiotic, and therefore unnecessary. It is only to encourage the old, dark, dead creeds into galvanic life. You cannot possibly gain aught by such a proceeding.'

He listened to pure reason for a moment, and then looked at Hel's eyes. They looked anxious, interested, and blue. There is nothing in pure reason that tells why one will obey eyes like these, and disobey if they be reddish, with white lashes and red lids. The result of the conflict was what it always has been when antagonism has existed between a girl's eyes and pure reason on a young man's mind. Pure reason was invited to go to the devil. Laurence's reply was:

'Will you read Goethe?'

'Yes; if you will make it a bargain.'

'Very well, I am ready to come to church. We will see which wins.' He thought to himself, 'church or Goethe.'

'Shall we go to-night?' said Jack. 'No one but ourselves will be going from the house, and we shall be able to do comfortably, and have a moonlight evening to look at.'

'You must not miss this fir-grove by moonlight, Mr. Laurence,' said Hel. 'It will be still more like Germany then.'

'I wasn't aware that Germany lay under a perpetual moonlight,' said Jack.

'It is said to be the mother-land of moonshine,' observed Max. 'Read Hegel, and you will be convinced.'

Maximilian Laurence and Helen Miller —each was a new experience to the other, and likely to be such continually, in consequence of some newly apparent quality or feature in either, which only appeared when summoned by occasion.

He was so entirely different to all the young men she had known, who were principally young officers in regiments stationed at Winterdale, and curates. The fact that it was almost exclusively tot hes e that he was compared and contrasted was naturally much to Laurence's advantage.

He had brought new elements into conversation, which was always a relief at Winterdale, where the barometer (known of course as the 'glass'), and approaching or past dances, and remarks about the peculiarities of appearance and conduct of

one's neighbours, were the prevailing ingredients of social intercourse. He appeared to Hel as one a long way above
her in the intellectual world, and a person
of some condescension to talk to her about
Rhine stories and church decorations,
when he might have talked to the Professor, or even Jack, about bones, or
Hegel, or something more congenial to his
mental tastes, and more on his intellectual
level.

She still held to the doctrine of the
omniscience of papa in matters philosophic,
having had no opportunity of exercising
the critical faculty, from want of knowledge of the subjects. Jack she thought
clever, but a little too conscious of it, and
a little too fond of what he called ' sitting
on ' other people who were unfortunate
enough to differ from him in opinion ; but,
nevertheless, more fit than herself to converse with one like the young Anglo-

Magyar. The fact that the latter had a good-looking, as well as an intelligent face, probably had, after all, some undefined influence in his favour. Then came that sense of pity for one evidently ' brought up ' without any religion. Hel had no doubt he would be religious if it was only explained to him and put before him in an attractive form. She had unconsciously put before him religion in what he temporarily thought its most attractive form— herself. She hoped, however, by the seductions of Easter decoration, and Mr. Exeter's persuasive harangues (and her own influence, perhaps, a little), to effect a conversion. *Elle n'est pas la première.*

Laurence was almost for the first time brought into the society of a pure and innocent, and, one may add, a High Church, girl. The circumstances of his birth had excluded him from society in Vienna, and the opportunity of associating with English

ladies had never before been given to him
—at any rate, not for more than half an
hour at some garden-party at Oxbridge.
He was totally unaccustomed to making
conversation for the benefit of this special
form of audience, and thus talked in some
fashion as he might to another man,
which made a much better impression, in
all likelihood, than any attempt at choos-
ing topics presumably suitable to the tastes
and comprehension of a 'young lady.' Of
women he had known a good number, but
they were certainly neither religious, nor,
in the usually accepted senses of the words,
pure and innocent. Her religion interested
and amused him, and her little efforts at
conversation were flattering, as betraying a
sympathy for his condition.

They wandered along the sides of fields,
under the shades of tall hedges, talking of
everything under the sun, Laurence talking experiences of walking tours in the

more beautiful parts of Germany and
Austria, of mountain inns, and moun-
taineer and huntsman innkeepers, of
students sitting together in crowds, on the
green glades of the Thüringer Wald, among
the fir-trees, round wooden tables with huge
krugs of beer, and long pipes, singing a
chorus of farewell to the departing sun,
and shouting out their freedom and youth
and love to the listening starlight. Also
perhaps to the listening village girls, if
any. Then he talked of the Harz and
of the districts of Schirke and Elend,
where he had wandered with a friend the
whole night on the first of May, one year,
and described the appearance of the place,
and told the story of the Walpurgisnacht.

Jack made remarks now and then,
but was rather silent. Hel was much
interested. German student life was something distant, mediæval and romantic to
her, knowing it only by scraps of allusion

in novels, songs, and her father's occasional
anecdotes. Legends too, had a great
fascination for her, especially if well told ;
and Max's were always lucidly and gracefully told, with occasional interruption
from that dreadful realist Jack, who brought
down upon everything his irresistible sense
of the ridiculous.

So much time passed in this way that
the conversation was interrupted by a
sound in the distance, which at first was
mistaken for one of the numerous sheep-
bells, but which was found on nearer in-
vestigation to be produced by the Professor, who was standing on the lawn,
swinging the domestic tocsin, with some
vigour, to announce to straying members
of the household that the season of afternoon tea was come. Hel, Max and
Jack walked into the drawing-room, to
find there Mrs. Radford. Jack shook
hands with a well simulated appearance

of intense joy and cordiality, and 'Mr. Laurence' was introduced.

Mrs. Radford had several serious reasons for calling, on this particular afternoon. The principal was curiosity, to know something about the new young man. She participated in the very laudable desire for news, which was such a distinctive feature among the later Athenians, but did not possess that reverence for accuracy of detail, without which, the possession of new information, however desirable a thing in itself, may become not only a snare to the possessor, but a bane to society at large. In other words, Mrs. Radford delighted in accumulating hypotheses about her neighbours, and distributing them as facts. This sort of person is called a gossip by the vulgar and those of low culture. A liar by the very vulgar, and the utterly destitute of culture.

The Professor treated her with the

critical courtesy which is usually extended
to the circulators of myth in ancient literature, observing that she had an irresistible
sense of the value and charm of allegory
and fable, as tending to impart moral
lessons. Mrs. Miller, with her all pervading amiability, said she was a really good
and pious woman, though a little narrow-
minded; Jack, in heated moments, alluded
to her as ' that frightful old cat, Sapphira
Radford;' Hel had always instinctively
disliked her because she insisted from the
earliest day of acquaintance on kissing
that ' dear, pretty, creature,' (meaning her,
Hel).

Of course Mrs. Radford wished to know
who this young man was, staying apparently with the Millers. He was introduced to her as Mr. Maximilian Laurence.
This gave very little information. She
asked in a momentary lull of discourse if
he had recently arrived from abroad—with

the idea of a nobleman or prince in dis-
guise or exile flitting through her head.
Max replied in excellent English that he
had just arrived from Oxbridge, thus leaving his nature and antecedents still a matter
of speculation.   Mrs. Radford gave him up
for the present, and turned to other topics.

'Have you called on those Franklands,
Mrs. Miller?' she inquired.   'I have not
yet; though every one seems to.'

'Mrs. Frankland came with a letter of
introduction from my sister in Paris, so I
have naturally called.'

'Ah! then you can perhaps tell me,
which no one seems to know, who *is* Mrs.
Frankland?   I know they are American,
and they seem to like her; but that is
about the extent of my information.' (Mrs.
Radford was one of those people who
always use an ambiguous mixture of pro-
nouns.)

'Colonel Frankland was attached to the

American Legation in Paris before he died for some time. I do not know Mrs. Frankland very well yet; but I think she is very nice, and I think ladylike, though Americans *are* rather different from us in some things.'

Jack listened hard. He had intended to ask who these new people were who had arrived while he was up at Oxbridge.

'Yes, to be sure. I have seen very few, but they seem to have such strange ways of looking at some things. And the girl, now do you know, *is* she Miss Frankland ?—for, if so, she is *very* unlike her mother ! People say all sorts of things about her here, but I daresay without foundation. My servants have it that she was picked up in Paris, during the war, by Mrs. Frankland, and that she was seen carrying a flag amongst the Communists and all sorts of things, but one can't believe these things. I make it a rule never to believe gossip. I always tell my servants not to repeat things they hear in this way.'

The Professor chuckled grimly, and said :

'The young lady speaks very good American for a Parisian " petroleuse," and I do not know that there were any of that profession at the age of about thirteen, as she must have been at the time.'

'I think I can explain,' said Mrs. Miller. 'She is Mrs. Frankland's niece, daughter of her brother, Dr. Taylor, who lived in Paris.'

'Oh, indeed !' replied Mrs. Radford, apparently rather offended at the discovery of Miss Taylor's comparatively respectable origin. 'Well,' added she, 'I think we will call. Dear Arthur has been urging me to do so for some time ; and he generally has the right opinion after all, dear boy. I depend a good deal on him for advice.

He is going up for his examination next month. Mr. Croker, his tutor, says he is not certain of his passing ; but I know my boy best, and I have every confidence in him.'

Jack tried to remain perfectly grave. He was quite aware, as were most other people and Croker in particular, that 'Dear Arthur' was about as nearly an idiot as a legally sane person could be, and that Mrs. Radford always contrived, as she had in this case, to bring him into conversation, however inapropos he might at the moment be, and to dwell upon him for the rest of her visit. This aim Jack endeavoured to defeat, by asking if she had been to church that morning. She replied:

' I was at the cathedral ; but that is a question I might ask you, Master Jack. Were you at church ?'

Jack hated being called ' Master Jack' by Mrs. Radford. He subsequently said :

'I don't see why an old beast like
that should presume that, because she
has known you from infancy, she may say
any stupid impertinence she pleases on
that account. It's not the least funny,
and very ineffective, if she thinks it is
going to rouse my temper.'

This was exactly what it did. Jack replied
at this moment, in a matter of course,
cheerful tone, which he trusted would
irritate his interlocutrix :

'Oh no; I seldom go.'

Mrs. Radford became serious and said :

'Don't you think that is rather a bad
preparation for that Sabbath which we are
told will be eternal ?'

'But we aren't told it will be an English
Sabbath, or that the whole week will be
spent in a cathedral, listening to the sermons of bishops, the reading of canons,
and the singing of choirs in rhythmical
monotony.'

Mrs. Miller saw a storm was brewing, and said :

' Don't be silly, Jack ;' and then rapidly, to prevent Mrs. Radford's crushing rejoinder : ' Let me give you another cup of tea ?'

' Thank you ; I will take just one cup more.'

Max was talking to Hel quietly, and being told that afternoon tea was a usual meal in English families, and telling her how German families took meals. Hel felt slightly uncomfortable from the consciousness that Mrs. Radford had an eye upon her, and would talk about her in association with Laurence. This made her defiantly confidential and attentive to him, from a mere feeling of irritation.

It was a long time before the elimination of Mrs. Radford could be effected. She had a petition to the Home Secretary advising him, as he valued his position and the stability of the Cabinet, to at once suppress entirely what the document somewhat tautologically described as the vivisection of live animals. This was to be signed by women only she explained.

'Don't you allow children to sign it?' asked the Professor.

'Oh, I don't suppose the poor dear dogs and things will get much sympathy from you, Dr. Miller! But I thought Mrs. Miller and Miss Miller, and some of your servants might have a little more feeling. There is a pamphlet, Mrs. Miller, that ought to go with the petition; it has illustrations, which ought to convince anyone who hesitated to sign.' And she handed all the documents, which resided temporarily in her black reticule, to Mrs. Miller for inspection.

They certainly ought, as Mrs. Radford remarked, to have convinced any wavering sympathiser with the oppressed animal kingdom.

The doctor looked over his wife's shoulder at the heart-rending scenes of torture depicted, with a pleased smile, and remarked:

'I cannot help sympathising with the Romans, in their passion for gladiatorial shows. I am sure there is a subtle, strong, and strange charm in actual cruelty for cruelty's sake. I think I should like to have been a Spanish inquisitor. The only real gratification left to us, which you would take away, is the torture of animals, whether by physiologists or farmers, or fox-hunters. We shall soon only be able to gratify our tastes pictorially by the assistance of Gustave Doré and the *Police News.'*

Mrs. Miller trembled at this speech, and the transformations and developments which experience led her to foresee it would undergo, under the able and practised guidance of Mrs. Radford's tongue. Mrs. Miller respected public opinion, in matters not precisely what she would call 'of conscience.' Her husband did not, and amused himself in giving Mrs. Radford, who had a faint but irritating suspicion that she was being made fun of, opportunities of describing him in glowing Satanic colours, to the rather extensive circle of her acquaintance.

Jack simply looked the superb contempt which propriety prevented him from expressing otherwise than guardedly. Laura was being shown roses by Hel, and talking about them.

Mrs. Radford got up to go, after the doctor's startling remarks, anent the inquisition, looking rather warm—a phenomenon for which the tea and the east wind were perhaps responsible. Having ceremoniously conducted her to the door, and carefully shut it, Jack returned, performing a sort of *cancan diabolique* intended to express superabundant joy, and generally relieve his mind from the oppression and irritation under which it usually suffered, in the presence of their departing visitor. Hel made an onslaught on the piano, forgetful of the day, and began a vivacious mazurka.

Mrs. Miller mildly said : 'Hush, dear.'

Hel revolved on the stool and said :

'You must not suppose, Mr. Laurence, that all our friends are like that.'

'I think this lady was rather interesting,' he replied with a faint laugh.

'That's what I thought once, by Jove !' said Jack. 'It's wonderful how time tires us of things. What rather fetched me was her extreme curiosity to have details as to your individuality, Max. I am rather sorry I didn't give her some.'

'I am not.'

'How do you young people propose to amuse yourselves this evening ?' asked the doctor.

'By going to church, I believe,' said

Jack, ' for the edification of Max's Pagan
mind.   By the way, Hel, you had better
go and get ready, as your pleasing sex
generally takes some time to do so.   Put
that fur thing on your shoulders—it will
be cold coming back, and we shall have
a tendency to loiter and look at the moon,
and smoke pipes, I know.'

CHAPTER X.

WHAT JACK SAW IN CHURCH.

'Oh, she doth teach the torches to burn bright!'

THE evening saw Hel, Max, and Jack on
their way to church. They went out of
the firgrove by the gate, along a field path,
and through a long lane lined with larches
on either hand, through whose delicate
lace-like foliage the evening gold was
glimmering. It was now April, and the
sun had contracted the habit of setting
somewhere between six and seven. Rooks
were flying home, cawing with the ob-
trusive loudness and pertinacity which
those birds usually affect, under the im-

pression, apparently, that it is vitally important to make their conversation as public as possible. Several villagers were walking leisurely to church, in the picturesque Sunday garb of the British peasant, so suited to the sort of Sabbath he usually spends, consisting of very shiny black clothes, a tall hat, and a thick umbrella with a thin cane stalk, with a weak looking hooked handle. Jack, Hel, and Max walked in a row. Hel in the middle, listening to the mixture of sounds filling the air—cawings of rooks, singing of larks, and chimes of churches resounding faintly through the still evening air, all the way from Winterdale, to which the small edifice over which Mr. Exeter presided, replied with a rather weak, though determined and defiant tinkle.

Hel looked very pretty, with the green boughs above her, and the grass grown ground at her feet, with spots and flashes

and strokes of yellow horizontal sunlight
on her at intervals. She wore a black fur
tippet, which sat well on her rather square
shoulders, and harmonised pleasingly with
the dark green dress she wore, whose
train she bore in one hand, the other
being, of course, occupied with a prayer-
book.

Her face wore a rather happy expression. Why not? Was she not guid-
ing the pale and handsome world-tired
young heathen by her side into the ways
of righteousness and the paths of peace?
Though it must be acknowledged that she
was listening with interest to a story from
him at this moment of how the heroes of
the Nibelungen-Lied rode to rescue Kriem-
hilde, and how they accomplished their
task by miscellaneous and abundant slaugh-
ter, giving a ground for the minstrels to
construct the great epic of their death.

All this was enchanting, no doubt, but

scarcely a good preliminary for an Easter evening service.

Laurence now felt himself quite at home with Hel, and had lost his embarrassing fear of saying that which he ought not, finding it quite easy to converse with an intelligent young English girl, even when she lay under the disadvantages of comparative innocence and a sweet and amiable superstition.

Jack was knocking the vegetation about viciously with an ash stick, and wondering what had come over Max, to make him loiter off to church in this lamb-like manner, as a way of spending the best part of the evening.

It scarcely occurred to him that Hel, although his own sister, was not Max's sister.

'Don't suppose you will find the temptation sufficient to make you repeat the performance,' he observed; 'old Exeter

will be about up to' his usual form, I suppose, and launch out long paragraphs on
the inimitable virtues of the early Fathers,
and the by no means inimitable vices of
modern sons.'

' Which to you, Jack, will of course be
painfully personal,' said Hel, laughing.

' It think it is a pity,' went on Jack,
' that some of those later Roman emperors
did not carry out the principle of perse-
cution more widely and systematically, and
thus have taken away from sensible young
men like St. Augustine the opportunity of
degenerating in later life into " Fathers,"
and flooding the world with their uninteresting opinions.'

' They have their revenge now,' said
Max ; ' the latter-day heathen, that once
were the stronger party, have to listen
patiently to quotations from the men
whom their spiritual ancestors would have
suppressed promptly with pitch, straw and

sulphur, or any other of those devices that their talented minds were so rich in.'

'It was Nero, wasn't it,' said Hel, 'that used to burn people with straw and sulphur ?'

'I believe so,' replied Max. 'He was not a lovable character, though some were of the contrary opinion at the time.'

'Still, there is something rather magnificent, though no doubt horrible, about him,' said Jack. 'I can easily imagine the ladies of the period to have all had a sort of sneaking admiration for Nero, uttered or unexpressed—principally the latter.'

'Here we are at church,' said Hel; 'Perhaps we shall hear some more about it.'

'Take a farewell look at the sunlight !' exclaimed Jack, as he removed his hat.

'Hullo, Miller !' said a voice in the porch. 'Didn't know you went in for church.'

Jack turned round and observed the

solid form and brick-coloured face of young
Radford, who has been already partially
alluded to under the title of 'dear
Arthur.'

'Well, I don't go in for it as a rule, but
I am going in to it now. How are you?
How's the General?'

'Oh, I'm all right, so is the governor.
Croker is going to preach to-night, so I
thought he'd like me to come.' Generous
young man, to sacrifice yourself to please
your poor hard-working curate-coach!
Artful young man, to apologise and
invent a motive for your presence!

'I am sure Croker will consider it a
graceful attention,' said Jack, as he followed
his sister into the church. 'By Jove!'
whispered he to young Radford, 'who is
that?'

'Who? Where?' replied he, in a very
audible tone, with the true tact of British
youth. 'Oh! that's those American

people, I believe,' he added, in a tone of uninterested uncertainty.

' I see,' said Jack, as they walked up the aisle. 'Well, I must go to my stall. See you between the acts. Hope you'll enjoy Croker's discourse.'

'What the devil brings Jack Miller and that other fellow here? I wonder who the other fellow is. Some beastly clever London fellow, I suppose—intellect and all that!' were Mr. Arthur Radford's reflections, as he found a seat whence he could see 'those American people,' of whose identity he had just expressed a careless uncertainty.

It is perhaps almost superfluous to remark that they were what brought him to church, and that a desire to have his mind improved by the Rev. Chrysostom Croker was but a flimsy veil to conceal a deeper-rooted and more sentimental motive.

When Jack inquired ' Who is that?' in

a surprised tone, 'that' referred to a
young girl, sitting beside a lady not precisely young, but scarcely old enough to be
the parent of her seventeen-year-old com-
panion. The older lady was Mrs. Frankland, relict of the late Colonel Frankland,
U.S.A., and was one of those graceful,
faded American women, of whom there
are so many, well-dressed, and possessing
marvellously minute hands and feet and
ears, and pretty fair hair, and having generally a rather foreign style and get-up. The
younger, Jack's 'that,' was a pale com-
plexioned girl, with clear brown eyes
with a slight brown tinge on the skin
round them, thin black eyebrows, and a
very pretty, rather 'decided' face, wearing, it must be remarked, rather a sulky
expression. Although evidently very
young, she was 'grown up,' and dressed
accordingly in a closely fitting dress of
black cashmere, and the only symptom of

juvenility about her was the fact that her curly black-brown hair was allowed to remain on her back, in the shape of a sort of half-open fan, being tied in at the back of her small sun-burnt neck with a piece of crimson ribbon.

She had taken off a long pair of black gloves, and was employing a pair of small tawny hands in abstracting bon-bons from a box which lay on the book-shelf in front of her. Jack called Max's attention to her, who looked at her awhile, and then said :

'Half kitten and half snake. "Hüt' dich, mein Freund, vor grimmen Teufels Fratzen. Doch schlimmer sind die sanften Engelsfrätzchen."'

This was Rosa.

Mr. Croker's sermon may have been distinctly edifying, and may have contained new facts, new ideas, and new opinions of the greatest solemnity and significance, though it is highly probable,

judging from precedent, that it was nothing
of the sort. Either way, it was entirely
thrown away upon Jack, as well as on
Mr. Arthur Radford, in spite of its having
been the ostensible inducement to the
latter to come to church; for neither of
them had the slightest idea what it had
been about when they came out. Jack
said to Hel, as soon as they got outside
the door :

'They are coming to dine with us, I
think some one said, aren't they ?'

'Who ? Oh yes! Those American
people. To-morrow. You noticed them
in church, I suppose ?'

'Yes. "Dear Arthur" called my attention to them. I suppose he is awfully
gone on the girl—Miss Frankland ?'

'Miss Taylor. I really don't know,
I can't say that I feel much interest in his
attachments. I shouldn't wonder if you
were "awfully gone" on her yourself soon.'

'What a charming sunset it is!' observed Jack in reply.

It was. It consisted of a glowing golden ground, cross streaked by numerous narrow nebulous grey and purple bars of many shades and shapes, finding their way into the south-western blue, on the one side, and the northern leaden grey on the other. Laurence was gazing abstractedly into it, looking apparently for something he had lost there. He was suddenly brought back again to earth by a question from Hel.

'Mr. Laurence!'

'Fräulein?'

'How did you like the service?'

'That is a difficult question to entirely answer. I have not been able to completely analyse my opinions and reduce them to intelligibility, or to separate the accidental from the essential features of the entertainment, as it is one to which I am not accustomed.'

'But why do you call it an entertainment?'

'I certainly should not find it one if I
went often, I think. For once, and that
for the first time, I did think it rather
amusing. But the decorations were exceedingly tasteful and charming, especially those in the neighbourhood of the
orchestra.'

'Choir, please. Mr. Laurence, this is
perfectly shocking.'

His remark was satisfactory in one sense,
though not in another.

Though Hel regretted the lack of
impression the service and poor Croker's
sermon had made on Max—and unfor-
tunately, on this occasion, on herself—she
was pleased by his praise of the 'orchestra'
decorations, being naturally unaware that
he had carefully ascertained from Jack
what share she had herself taken in the
adorning of the church.

'I am afraid it is,' replied he; 'I certainly feel more moved by that sky than anything I have heard this evening in the church.'

'A sky like that,' said Jack, 'always makes me despair of ever being able to paint.'

'It is wonderful how intimately associated with the joy and sorrow of one's life the sky becomes,' observed Laurence.

'You speak as if you had known both?'

'I have had a little of both. I have often sought the one—I have often found the other. Do you know the lines of the song—

'"Man schafft so gern nach Sorg' und Müh',
    Sucht Dornen auf, und findet sie"?'

'Oh yes! It always seemed to me that most of those German songs were very sentimental and unreal, though they have very pretty tunes, it is true.'

'You find that? I congratulate you. Many of us find them only too real.'

'Do you ever write songs?' asked Hel suddenly, while Jack was staying behind to light a pipe.

Max looked into her blue eyes, with their interested expression of inquiry, and said :

'Sometimes.'

'Are they visible to the public?'

'They are. They exist in print on a remote bookseller's shelves in London, and thence they disappear very slowly. I fancy you would call them sentimental and unreal, and they have not the compensating advantage of tunes.'

'You must give me an opportunity of judging for myself.'

'Thank you, I will.'

Jack's prediction concerning the probability of the evening being spent in loitering and smoking was distinctly fulfilled.

Hel suggested of her own accord that they should go for a short walk. Max said he should like to see the country under the evening light. So they walked over fields, and alongside hedges, and under trees, listening for nightingales, which were to be heard in large numbers at this time of the year, and talking of various things, Laurence being the principal speaker, as Hel had more interest in listening, and had not quite so much to say, and not quite as large an experience to extract illustrations from. Jack pulled away silently at a pipe, which gave out a gurgling sound at every suck, and had small beady drops of liquid matter on the outside. Hel said it was a horrid thing. Jack retorted that it was ' Fine !' Jack was not communicative. At last he inquired :

' Who is coming to dinner to-morrow besides these Americans ?'

'Mr. Exeter.'

'Ah, of course! I might have guessed that. I wonder if we could give a dinner, if we tried, without asking him? Not that he lends any lustre to the entertainment.'

'He is a very good man.'

'Possibly. But he is not amusing, except in the pulpit.'

'Well, it is not the whole duty of a rector to amuse you.'

'Hang the rector! What is the "front name" of that little American girl?'

'I don't know. You had better ask her to-morrow.'

'I will.'

'Your brother seems very much struck with this young lady,' observed Max.

'Oh, he always is with every new face he sees.'

'I wonder a girl of your pious up-bringing does not draw the line at least at perjury,' said Jack.

Thus they walked on, until the moon became very brilliant and the sky very pale, with purple clouds streaked across it. This was all that remained of that flaming golden sunset with grey bars. Hel gave the word of command to go back to Eave Lodge. Max went into low-voiced, confidential raptures over the beauties of the scene, and Hel looked at his face and listened. He looked paler than ever in the twilight, and his eyes darker. He was rather like a marble Dionysos, with nineteenth century clothes on a Greek mind and body. Jack said he looked like an evil spirit who was meditating on passing an examination for re-admission to Paradise, and trying to assume the proper expression.

When they reached the house, Hel said :

'I am sure you must be hungry, Mr. Laurence. You have had a long walk, preceded by—an entertainment to which you are not accustomed,' she added, with a quiet and rather sly smile.

'Food had not entered into my head——'

'Mouth, you mean,' said Jack.

'Into my ideas, till you mentioned it. It has been a beautiful walk, and one I shall remember. The " entertainment " I shall hope to repeat some day.'

'Will you help me to translate some of Goethe to-morrow, if I find the book?' asked Hel shyly, as they went through the now darkened hall.

'Of course.'

CHAPTER XI.

ARTHUR RADFORD—MILES GLORIOSUS.

MRS. RADFORD was sitting at her Davenport writing letters, an occupation which generally occupied her Monday mornings. Very long letters they generally were, and crossed to a bewildering extent, for that mysterious reason that makes all women cross letters, although their means allow them unlimited supplies of paper. When Mrs. Radford wrote letters, Winterdale might tremble. The amount of extraordinary information, usually of a personal and unreliable nature, conveyed about the British Isles by that fine, sloping, neat,

illegible hand-writing, was something startling. People discussed the eccentricities
of Winterdale on Tuesdays in Tunbridge
Wells, in Bath, in Clifton, in Ryde, and
in all places where people are idle and un-
intelligent, and take an interest in the moral
dissection of their acquaintances, thanks
to this indefatigable correspondent. On
Wednesday or Thursday they discussed
them at Cannes, and Nice, and Baden-
Baden. In a few weeks they discussed
them at Simla and Puna. Mrs. Radford
might have called herself an ' Agency for
the Dissemination of Unreliable Information.'

Her son, Arthur, was sitting in an arm-
chair, gazing steadily at a book which
endeavoured to make clear the to him
incomprehensible and vindictively various
peculiarities of ' similar triangles.' Arthur
really deserves some notice, if not pity.
He had been what is customarily called

15—2

educated in England at a public school, and had been two years at Camford, where he had succeeded, after great struggles, in passing 'Mods,' which would save him his preliminary examination for the army. His friends there had nicknamed him the 'Muscular Christian.' There is no denying that they were justified in using the first adjective. He once ran a narrow risk of rowing in the University eight, and was great in football, cricket and athletics, appearing occasionally at Winterdale sports in costumes of striking colours, and doing unheard-of things in high jumps.

It was perhaps unfortunate that the physical element had predominated over the mental in his education; but that was better than having neither. Not only Latin, and Greek, and mathematics, but ordinary literature, in most of its aspects, with the exception of a certain class of novels and newspapers, dealing largely in technical sporting terms, and 'incidents of flood and field,' were to him unfamiliar, and by him unappreciated.

Society, in its usually accepted sense, was not his element.

Of ladies he was possessed as a rule of a wholesome dread, and was usually dumb in their presence, oppressed by the consciousness that they must be either laughing at him, or 'pumping' him, or shocked at him. This was, indeed, frequently the case. He had gradually formed an opinion—and when Arthur Radford took the effort to form an opinion, no power, natural or supernatural, could alter it—that if 'ladies,' were replaced by barmaids —with bars—in the circle in which he moved, life, freed from the galling restraint of conventionality and decorum, would be far more worth living.

The greatest failing in his philosophy of

life, and the one which caused him even more mental discomfort and disappointment than even the slowness of development of his moustache, was the firm conviction that the ' world was his oyster,' and no one else's oyster, and only an oyster. His own self and the oyster were a life-long antithesis. He consumed the beer, beef and tobacco of the oyster, and gave it nothing in return. It laughed, knowing that it would laugh last, by-and-by.

Arthur considered himself the important side of the antithesis. The oyster was of the contrary opinion, and in its eternal god-like scorn laughed on, contenting itself with occasionally nipping him between the shells.

In plain English, Arthur Radford was rather selfish, rather conceited, and rather stupid, and was by no means unique among young Englishmen in those respects.

He was rather a trial to Jack Miller, who was impulsive, and careless about the effect of his words, as long as he thought them pointed, or neatly scornful, and sometimes very nearly roused the abusive wrath of Arthur, whom of course he had known from their not-far-distant boyhood. They quarrelled on an average about once a week, and made it up, and smoked pipes and played billiards after.

Arthur, having one of those minds which are so constituted as to be independent of such terrestrial restrictions as logic, thought fit, in spite of this, to indulge frequently and fiercely in political discussions, and to advertise his opinions in a dogmatic and challengeful manner. He stated that he was a Conservative, and nothing annoyed and puzzled him so much as the cheerful way in which Jack, and sometimes Dr. Miller, played conversational 'tip-cat' with Church and State, and all the institutions which he held in deepest reverence —the English public schools and Universities, for example.

Arthur, with all his short-sightedness for the nature and merits of others, was obliged to admit to himself that Jack was clever, after his fashion, and knew and spoke of topics which were as cuneiform inscriptions to him.

He had a firm belief in consistency, as a virtue by itself. Consequently his opinions resembled, as has been hinted, those often-quoted laws of the Medes and Persians. The proposition that it may be sometimes consistent to change a belief, he regarded as a subtle and dangerous sophism. He was much distracted by the freedom of speech which Jack permitted himself in political and religious questions, and would listen to some half-nonsensical, half-serious tirade of the latter against some respectable and recognised principle, which he

(Jack) would be heard vigorously defending a week afterwards, and reproduce it triumphantly, and brandish it in his antagonist's face, with the prelude :

'Why, the other day you were saying——'

On which Jack would reply : 'Was I ? What then ?'

This crippled Arthur momentarily. He would soon, however, retort :

'Well, which do you expect us to believe ?' and look round for applause at his artful dilemma.

'Whichever you like.'

'But don't you mean what you say ?'

'I have never completely satisfied myself on that point. I generally leave it to the person I am talking to, to find out.'

'Well then, I suppose you don't care whether you are telling the truth or not ?'

This gratuitous assumption indicated rapid rise of temper on Arthur's part, and that a consequent descent to personalities might be expected.

'What is the particular object of telling the truth ? We should lose an immense deal of the charm of this life if everyone did. Fancy if no one said anything that he did not know to be true! Results : sudden disappearance of novels, " latest intelligence," and " special correspondence ;" dead silence at afternoon teas and Dorcas meetings ; total cessation of compliment and civility in conversation. Some will say that there would be indisputably beneficial results, for instance—sermons would dwindle ; speeches in the Houses of Legislature would be shorter ; promises would cease to be made by candidates to constituencies. In a general way, there would be a refreshing silence about the wide earth, wherein one could more easily pursue intellectual occupations.'

'Do you mean that you think it would

be a bad thing or a good thing if everyone
spoke the truth?' Arthur would persist,
with terrifically literal straightforwardness,
having in his head the beginning of the
discussion, which Jack certainly had not.

' "That," as the cabmen say, " I leaves
to you." I have put both sides before
you, like an advocate. You, with the
superior dignity of judge, must choose
between them. By the way, under our
reign of truth, real advocates would have
to shut their " traps" a good deal, wouldn't
they?'

This is a comparatively peaceful example
of the sparring and baiting which went
on frequently between the two. Under
strong stimulation, Arthur was capable
of pouring out torrents of incoherent
wrath from those conversational reservoirs
which answer very much to the concise
and graceful metaphor of ' vials.'

It is now only due to him to state that

he was a very hardworking, honest fellow, who never had told a lie since boyhood — at least, very seldom ; who was afraid of nothing in this world, and would probably make a capital soldier if the inquisitors of the Civil Service Commission permitted him to become one ; that he had a bass voice and could sing music-hall songs (and practised them alone, in secluded woods, with the 'spokens'), and had a very grateful and amiable disposition, though his wrath was easily evoked. Just now he was in a new and peculiar condition. He yawned, and put his Euclid face downwards on a footstool, and said :

' Mother !'

' Yes, dear.'

' Have you called on the Franklands yet ?'

' The who, dear ? Oh, those American people !—no, not yet.'

' Then why the—— I mean, why don't you ?'

'I don't think there is any hurry. You
see, I hardly know who they are yet.'

'Well, it's not for want of asking, anyhow.'

'That is rude and uncalled-for, Arthur.
If I like to be sure that my acquaintances
are proper sort of people, I think it is only
right. Besides, they have hardly had
time to settle down yet.'

'I don't know what you mean by
"settling down." They have had time
to go and see the Millers and go to
church, and go out walks and buy things
in the shops in Winterdale. The Millers
seem to think them all right. They have
asked them to dinner to-night.'

'The Millers are excellent people, but
they have very strange ideas.'

'Well, they've *got* some ideas! Wish I
had Jack's head for some things.'

Mrs. Radford's maternal pride was fired:
'I'm sure, dear, you could do very well if

you tried.   I hope you will never grow up
like young Miller. He has very loose
ideas, and an impertinent mocking way of
expressing them, which gives a very bad
impression. He has a reckless, dissipated
appearance——'

'Oh, come now, draw it mild, mother!'

'I repeat it. I am very sorry for him,
continued Mrs. Radford, in a cheerful tone,
'and for his mother. Do you know who
that strange-looking young man with
them is?'

'Queer, long-haired, pallid fellow? No,
not the least. Some Oxbridge-man —
hasn't quite got the " 'Varsity" cut about
him—at least, *our* " 'Varsity" cut.'

'No, dear, he has not. Miss Hel seems
to find something in him, though.'

'Well, about the Franklands. They
have heaps of tin, I know. I was talking
to——a fellow in Winterdale' (Arthur just
prevented himself from saying 'the bil-

liard-marker' in time), 'who told me they
had made the house they've taken quite
different inside, and brought all sorts of
rum foreign things into it.'

'Money ? Things in the house ? Ah !
to be sure ; Americans in Europe generally
are rich. The best classes are the ones
that come across the Atlantic. I always
thought Mrs. Frankland a very lady-like,
distinguished-looking person.'

'Did you ?' said Arthur, in a tone of
innocent wonderment at his parent's
changed tone—the result of his accidental
lucky hit of the billiard-marker's information. Arthur was not diplomatist enough
to have said that on purpose.

'Yes. I think we might call soon.'

'All right,' in a tone of suppressed glee.
'What awful rot Euclid is !'

As may be without difficulty divined,
Arthur had conceived a silent passion for
Rosa.

Indeed, he had some excuse. Having seen nothing but barmaids and the young ladies of the neighbourhood, who were, with the exception of Hel, not very attractive, it is not surprising if he fell in love, to such extent as his matter-of-fact soul was able, with the rare and to the sense enticing little morsel of humanity put before him. He had a notion of getting acquainted with her before Jack had had the opportunity to do so, which would give him, as it were, a starting handicap, in case Jack should feel attracted in the same direction. He intended to strike while the iron was hot, and induce his mother to call, of course with him, that very afternoon.

We will now, with the kind permission of the reader, change the scene to the sitting - room of Seymour Villa, Mrs. Frankland's new habitation. The time is early on the same afternoon. It is a very

warm April Monday. The room was exceedingly attractive and cool-looking. The
walls were dark green, with yellowish-
brown 'decorative' flowers, with very long
stalks and very curious leaves, wandering
almost imperceptibly over it, and bore
several small and strange pictures, mostly
the work of Paul Félix and brother artists.
The French windows were wide open, and
displayed a fringe of white roses round
their apertures, and a pretty sloping lawn,
covered with yew and cypress, bushes of
lilac and trees of laburnum, under which
were chairs of comfortable form, apparently
sunning themselves.

In the room Mrs. Frankland was sitting
at a grand piano, playing through Gounod's
'Faust' with practised hands. On a dark
green velvet sofa, Rosa, in a black dress,
with her hair in an untidy but charming
curly mat, was lazily lying, smoking
cigarettes, and watching white clouds

wander slowly over the blue sky, occasionally taking gulps of very strong black coffee from a very pretty Dresden cup, intermittently with sips of maraschino from a liqueur glass.

Mrs. Frankland left off playing, and said :

'Say, Rosie, give me another cup, will you ?'

Rosa, after a moment's pause, rose and poured out the desired coffee, and brought it over to the piano. Mrs. Frankland added :

'Sorry to run against your principle of not making yourself useful, of course. Wonder what these English neighbours of ours would say, if they came and found us living like this ?'

'It don't much matter, anyway, what they would say or think,' replied Rosa.

Her French accent was getting almost entirely obliterated, and being replaced by

the American one of Ivor Taylor and his
sister. Sometimes the two mixed themselves curiously together. Rosa replaced
herself on the couch, and said :

‘ I’ve never been to an English dinner-
party before. What is it like ? The books
describe it as very stupid.’

‘ It isn’t *la vie de Bohème* certainly,
but I expect it won’t be bad *chez* these
Millers. They seem very good sort of
people. If they don’t invite any of the
inhabitants here, it will be enjoyable. I
rather hope that absurd rector will come,
though. He is entertaining. I like to
shock him mildly now and then. That
girl of the Millers is pretty, isn’t she ?’

‘ Yes. I suppose that was her brother
in church yesterday—the fair one of those
two young men that were with her. He
is good-looking too.’

‘ Is he ? I didn’t look. I don’t believe
you ever do anything but look for good-

looking young men's faces in church, Rosie.'

' What else is there to do ? But I don't find them here much, anyhow. Mr. Miller—if that's him—looks nice. I expect he would be rather jolly to talk to.'

' Well, you will find out to-night. He is safe to take you in to dinner.'

Here a ring at the bell was heard.

' Do for gracious sake, Rosie, get off that sofa, and make yourself a little less like a tame panther ! There's some one calling. Throw that cigarette away.'

' It don't matter if they do see me smoking,' replied Rosa, at the same time, however, obeying. ' If people disapprove of one for things like that, they can't be worth much for friends, anyway.'

'Mrs. and Mr. Radford ' were announced as the door opened, and Arthur was introduced to the new world.

Mrs. Radford began with the time-honoured common-place of first visits anent the weather and the neighbourhood and hoped she did not in any way disturb Mrs. Frankland, who replied :

'Oh, not in the least. We were just in that stage of languid stupidity which one generally gets into after a late breakfast' (it was half past two), 'and are only too glad to see some friends to arouse our sleeping intellects.'

Mrs. Radford opened her eyes at the word 'breakfast,' and said :

' I suppose you have been accustomed to keeping very late hours in Paris ?'

'Why, yes. You see one seldom gets to bed there before one or two ; and here, although there is no particular reason for sitting up late, one does it out of habit, and from inability to sleep early. Very sad, isn't it ?'

' Well, we are all rather early here,

except, perhaps, the Millers. I think you know them? And they are out, I believe, at all sorts of strange hours, when the stars are out, and everyone else is in bed and asleep, or——'

'Or ought to be?' added Mrs. Frankland, smiling. 'Well, I am afraid our habits are rather irregular. I confess I am glad to find that there is some one else rather like us in that way here; one won't feel so kind of strange and Bohemian.'

'Oh, I think it is quite interesting,' said Mrs. Radford, who was willing to excuse anybody's eccentricities who could afford to have them.

Rosa was entertaining Arthur, and on discovering that he was reading for the army—a piece of information he thought fit to volunteer, said:

'Oh, I like soldiers awfully; if I had been a man, I should have gone into the army.'

The young soldier *in posse* appropriated this compliment to soldiers *in esse* to himself, and radiated all over, only to be morally snuffed out by the next question:

'Do you know young Mr. Miller?'

'Oh yes—great pal of mine!'

'Really! What does he do? Is he going into the army too?'

'No. He is a sort of medical student. He has taken his degree at Oxbridge.'

'Oh, I shall enjoy getting to know English students. I have spent a good many years with Paris students—jolly fellows!'

'What *can* she mean?' thought Arthur.

'Do you like Mr. Miller? What sort of a fellow is he?'

'Clever kind of a chap; but he is rather a rum sort. I believe he is rather fast. My mother says he looks reckless and dissipated.' Arthur was rather given to making statements beginning with ' My mother says.' ' He doesn't care much what he says or does.'

Arthur's generously conceived attempt to prepossess Rosa against Jack did not meet with entire success.

' I like men like that—not afraid to join in any sort of lark, I suppose ?'

' Oh no ; I believe he spent most of his time at Oxbridge in " joining in larks." He knows a lot, and could pass exams., and have plenty of time to muck about as well.'

' Now, do please tell me, Mr. Radford, what is Oxbridge, and what is " mucking about ?" '

Arthur opened his eyes and mouth at this unheard-of ignorance.

' You know I am in England for the first time, and want to know all about everything.'

' Oh, Oxbridge is the university.　The

other one, you know,' remarked Arthur lucidly.

' I see. I guess " mucking about " is English for knocking around, isn't it ?'

' Very likely.'

Arthur was getting rather tired of conversation on Jack Miller. It was cruel of Rosa ; but then she did not know, and if she had known, would not have particularly cared.

' What a charming place this is !' said Mrs. Radford. ' I have never been here before.'

' Well, I hope you'll come again, Mrs. Radford,' said Mrs. Frankland, good-naturedly. ' We have very few friends at present here.'

' I hope we shall see you at our place soon, when you have had a little more time to look about you. I dare say you will find the neighbours a little cold and restrained at first. They generally are with strangers.'

'Well, I guess we'll bear it. We have the Millers, who are among the best people I've ever met in England—not much of the Continental ideal of the English about them.'

'No, indeed. They are old friends of ours; though I can't help saying' ('Why can't you help it?' thought Mrs. Frankland) 'that the children have been rather loosely brought up. It is a pity.'

'Oh, do you think that? I thought Miss Miller looked quite a sweet girl, and the pink of propriety, when her mother brought her round here. To be sure, I don't know anything about the young man. Young men are always odd creatures. But I know nothing against him.'

'Jack is a dear good fellow, isn't he, Arthur?' said Mrs. Radford.

Arthur gave a languid 'Yes.' It was fated apparently that everyone should din the merits of Jack Miller into his ears.

'But,' continued Mrs. Radford, whose praise was invariably followed by a 'but,' 'he is a little too old for his age, and has lived a little too much from home, I think. He seldom goes to church, and I believe has very loose views on very serious subjects. So, for the matter of that, has Dr. Miller, though of course, for him, poor man, it is different. Still, there is always the responsibility, and then it is such a pity, for they are really nice people, and very well off.'

'Good gracious!' silently ejaculated Mrs. Frankland. Audibly, she said:

'Can't Rosie give you some coffee, Mrs. Radford?'

Mrs. Radford, who never eat or drank between meals 'on principle,' declined with thanks. Arthur, to his own and his mother's surprise, had the audacity to accept. How could he refuse when Rosa said:

'You are going to have some, aren't you?' with the coffee-pot in her small sun-tanned hands? He looked round for the milk, and not seeing any, silently resigned himself to the novel sensation of *café noir* (the coffee provided by Mrs. Radford at breakfast being of the wateriest and milkiest description, also 'on principle'), looking forward to a subsequent discourse from his mother on the unhealthy effects of strong coffee on the nerves and body generally. He fortified himself for this with a glass of maraschino. Rosa smiled, and remarked to herself 'Duffer!' as she saw him blink at the first mouthful. She was restraining herself with difficulty from beginning a second cigarette out of pure defiance. Mrs. Radford, at this stage of the proceed-

ings, thought fit to withdraw herself and
son, who departed with obvious unwilling-
ness, and ventured, on the strength of the
maraschino, to say to Rosa he hoped to
see her again soon, to which she replied :

'Oh, you're sure to see lots of us. We
are going to be here some time—good-
bye.'

Mrs. Radford disapproved of Rosa all
the way home, and discovered that her
heels were absurdly high, and stated the
important æsthetic fact that when she was
a girl (Arthur was used to references to
this rather remote period, as a criterion for
everything in feminine manners and costumes) young ladies never wore their hair
in untidy fringes on the tops of their heads.
Arthur silently wished that there were
more heels (and feet generally) like those
in Winterdale, and that Jack Miller had

obtained the position of physician-in-or-
dinary to the Emperor of Brazil, involving
immediate residence in that or any other
remote and antipodal land.

END OF VOL. I.

BILLING AND SONS, PRINTERS, GUILDFORD AND LONDON.

www.ingramcontent.com/pod-product-compliance
Lightning Source LLC
Chambersburg PA
CBHW031346020726
47499CB00005B/1417

9 783337 053383